All Rights Reserved

The Piggy Farmer

Emmy Ellis

A Word of Advice, Cass

"There have been times I've kept shit to myself. Didn't want to burden your mam, see. The thing is, if you let people know everything about you, they've got you trapped. Keep something back, always. Besides, it adds a bit of mystery to you. Folks get intrigued, they want to know what you're hiding, figure you out like you're some kind of riddle, and that's when you'll spot the ones who just want info from you. They'll stand out a mile once you twig. I hope you never get shafted, but it's inevitable. I only hope I'm around to see them off. I'd kill anyone who hurt you. If I'm not there...well, you know what to do. Fucking kill them yourself."

– Lenny Grafton, ex-leader of the Barrington

Dear Diary

*A*ll this crap with the Jade has shown me I can't trust anyone—even Mam was hiding stuff from me. Finding out via that diary what she used to get up to… I know she's entitled to her secrets, but for me to not have known she'd gadded about with Dad, helping him keep the patch in order…

She's killed people, helped make them disappear.

Fucking hell.

Maybe Dad had told <u>her</u> to keep something of herself back, too.

At least I know now. I can count on Mam to help me like she did with Karen and Zhang Wei. For all I know, she's been suppressed all these years, looking after me instead of being in the thick of it. Why didn't she go back to doing her thing once I was an adult?

Dad probably said no.

He said a lot of things.

He <u>didn't</u> say a lot of things, too.

I'm fast learning that his advice went deep when he took it himself. He kept <u>a lot</u> back, not just 'something'. I'm wondering now whether he only showed us a percentage of himself. Maybe fifty. The other half…God knows what we're unaware of. I get why he kept Doreen's secret, but to not even put it in the ledgers?

And as for Doreen... She committed the act of murder with intent. She didn't hit Karen over the head like she had with Sharon's ex, she stabbed the shit out of Karen's face and slit the woman's throat, for God's sake.

Should I ask her to be my right hand?

Or is Mam the one I need by my side?

Chapter One

Cassie was in the same situation as when she'd been staring at Jiang on the concrete round the back of the Jade. Here she was, presented with a body in a car boot, except this time, it was going to be dodgy as eff covering it up. A risk.

Lou Wilson had killed a copper. PC Bob Holworth's face, squashed, had a tyre mark across it. He didn't appear to have much of his brains left, like the top of his head had exploded from the pressure of the weight when she'd run him over. At least Cassie assumed that was what had happened.

What had Lou been *doing* out in the middle of the night? Cassie, Mam, and Doreen had left her at Handel Farm after they'd taken Karen's and Zhang Wei's minced-up bodies to the barn for the pigs to eat. Lou must have waited for her husband, Joe, to fall asleep, then went out and did…this.

A chill wind sliced across the back of Cassie's neck, creating a ripple of shivers down her spine. From the darkened driveway, she glanced at the upstairs windows. No lights. Only the one on the porch glowed, something Mam kept on if Cassie wasn't home yet. She shifted her sights to her flat above the garage.

She'd move back in there soon.

She was knackered—it had been a bloody long day—and she'd arrived home from torturing her useless right hand, Jason, to fill in the ledger then go to bed. Instead, she stood beside a creepy-as-fuck Lou, who'd gone even weirder than she usually was.

Cassie recalled their recent conversation and looked in the boot, cringing. The interior light showcased blood and brain matter on the dark-grey carpet and Bob curled into a pretzel where Lou had somehow packed him inside. Killing a police officer was bad news.

"You said you're 'The Piggy Farmer'." Cassie closed the boot—she didn't need any nosy neighbours clocking a dead uniformed officer, and besides, she couldn't stand looking at him any longer. She'd need to warn residents to keep their gobs shut if they spotted Bob, and quite frankly, she couldn't be arsed. "You also said you want to kill all the police who were involved with Jess' disappearance."

Everyone knew Lou still hadn't got over the murder of her three-year-old daughter, but for fuck's sake, killing coppers? Why now, all these years later? What had happened in Lou's brain for her to snap like this? Or had she always planned to do it and had bided her time, waiting for courage to lend her a hand?

Lou's face was shrouded by darkness, meaning Cassie didn't have to see her eerie face, thank God.

"I've been thinking about it for years, and now I'm ready. Like I told you, your mam's in on it. She understands I can't sit back and do nowt."

"Why didn't you do it sooner?"

"Because it only came to light recently that Lenny fucked up, that's why. The Mechanic didn't kill my girl, Vance Johnson did. I convinced myself back then that so long as one of the kidnappers was dead, some form of justice had been served. Now, knowing *both* people hadn't been caught? Those coppers were just as clueless as your old man. God rest his soul and everything, but fucking hell."

Cassie couldn't argue there. Dad had well messed up. It was hard for her to cope with his pedestal crumbling. At first, she'd been embarrassed at his mistake, wanted to cover it up, but soon after, anger had taken over. He wasn't the man she'd thought, and she felt lied to. Duped.

She sighed. "But the pigs still fucked up back then, and you knew it, Lou."

"The Vance business brought it all back. It was like the scab had been picked off."

You've picked it enough yourself for twenty-odd years. You never let the wound heal. "So what do you plan to do, go round running them all over?" Cassie imagined the shite left on the road, evidence Lou had mown down a copper—the one who'd kept his mouth shut and turned a blind eye on the Barrington. The man who Cassie needed on her side. Now she'd have to feel out whoever replaced Bob on the community beat and see if they'd take a wedge of money each week to look the other way.

Things were getting more difficult by the day. Why did Dad have to go and die? While she'd allowed her inner monster to rule since the six months before he'd passed on, hiding her true self, could she continue to do that now the police were the targets? It was a strange quandary. She broke the law, but pissing about with coppers like this seemed wrong—more wrong than the other stuff she did.

'Business always comes first, Cass. You deal with shit and worry about it afterwards.'

Dad's voice didn't bring her comfort like it usually did. She was out of her depth here. Pigs would be swarming the area when Bob didn't check in, trying to find their colleague. They didn't warm to one of their own being killed in the line of duty. They'd pull out all the stops, and that would most likely piss Lou off an' all. Cassie could imagine it now: *Oh, they're out there looking for a cop killer, but they let my Jess' murderer wander round the country offing other kiddies. If they'd found him before he'd legged it, those children would still be alive.*

Plus, there was limited time to get the road cleared up. While it was winter, the mornings dark, someone would be out on their way to work soon.

"Where did you run him over?" Cassie hugged herself—not only because it was bloody cold, but for comfort. Did Mam know the method of death Lou had chosen? Had she agreed it was a good idea? Was there some of Bob's brains and blood in the tyre treads, transferring onto the driveway?

Lou sniffed. It was odd seeing her without her usual tartan blanket wrapped around her shoulders, a thick jacket in its place. "It wasn't a road. It was the parking area behind the meat factory."

Cassie's skin seemed to freeze, and anger boiled, soon warming her up, her face flaming. "What? The *factory*? For fuck's *sake*." She paced, in part to get away from Lou before she walloped her one, and also to think. Her mind raced. This was a right old dog's dinner. She returned to Lou, her fists balled. "One, he could have radioed in that he was going there, and two, why the hell was he poking around up that way? Did he see you? Like, did you follow right up his arse so he could have also radioed it in that you were there? He'd have seen your number plate."

A loud snort came from Lou's direction, spooky in the blackness, the hedge separating Mam's from next door a clumpy backdrop. "When he took the road to the factory, I carried on, did a U-turn, drove round the back, then ploughed into the fucker as he walked towards me."

And you have no guilt whatsoever by the sound of it.

It played out inside Cassie's head. Bob was an okay fella. As old as Lou, early retirement only a few years away. What bad luck to be killed when he'd almost finished his stint. "We're going to have to go there and clean up. I can't have any workers seeing blood and whatever in the snow. I assume his brains are on the ground."

"I picked up the big lumps and put them in a carrier bag. Joe's pigs will enjoy them."

Cassie closed her eyes at the image that presented. Lou getting enjoyment from holding someone's brain. Cassie opened them again and stared at the shadowed bushes to her right that split Mam's property from the public pavement, lowering her voice. "How the hell did you manage to get him into the boot?"

Lou was a wisp of a woman, barely eating since Jess had died, and although she worked on her husband's farm and must have decent muscles, she wasn't exactly weightlifter of the sodding year, was she.

"I got by fine, thanks very much. Anger lends a hand when you're so steaming with it you could explode."

Lou came off as demented, her voice holding a breathy quality, as if she'd lost the strength to speak properly, and Cassie supposed she would be crackers, given the circumstances, the road she'd travelled up until this point. To lose a child… Cassie couldn't imagine the pain the woman had been through, and she never would. Having kids wasn't on her agenda anymore, not now she did such a dangerous job. She wasn't like Mam, who'd given it all up for her kid, and despite Cassie being sickened sometimes as her old self, her new self, her inner monster, enjoyed what she did.

She slapped her thigh. "Right, we need to get Mam up. She can sort the copper with Marlene." Christ, a police officer going into the adapted mincer at the factory wasn't something Cassie had ever thought would happen. "We'll clean up the—" She paused, dread seeping into her. "Christ, Lou. His car!"

Lou laughed quietly, and the tinkle of it had the hairs on the back of Cassie's neck standing up.

"Already dealt with that."

"What?"

"I phoned your mam for help. She turned up at the factory and drove it way past the squat, about a mile farther on, and set it on fire. I followed, then took her back to pick hers up. We came here. I was about to go home but knocked on the door again—I couldn't risk Joe waking up and catching me putting the copper in one of the pig pens, so I wanted your mam to help me get rid of Bob. There's his uniform that needs burning… Then you came along."

That was something, the car being torched, and at least it was in the dark, out in the sticks, so it was unlikely anyone would see it unless they drove past or an insomniac looked out of a window and spotted the flames in the distance. But a mile away from the squat? That was far too close. Cassie had Jason pinned to the floor in there by an eight-inch nail through his shin, and Jimmy, her new grass, was babysitting him. She couldn't afford for the police to roll up at the abandoned house, asking questions once they'd discovered the blackened police car shell.

But would they even bother knocking? As far as they're aware, it's empty.

"Give me a second to think," she said. "Go and wake Mam—I'm assuming she went straight to bed, what with the house lights being off."

Cassie fired off a WhatsApp message to Jimmy: *Make sure the blackout blind in the living room is attached to the wall—there's Velcro on them. I forgot to tell you to do that when I was there. We can't let any light out. Shit's gone down. Don't open the door unless I get hold of you first. Did my fella come by with the telly and everything?*

Lou stood at the front door, and Cassie paced the driveway, then moved to the end of it and checked the street. No lights on anywhere apart from a porch down the way a bit.

Her phone bleeped, and she stood by Lou's car to read it.

Jimmy: *I already did the blind. Okay about opening the door. Yes to the telly and stuff. Your guest has passed out.*

Cassie: *Good. We don't need him waking up and creating noise. If he does, punch him until he blacks out again.*

Jimmy: *Right.*

Cassie wasn't sure Jimmy was up to that, but if he wanted to earn big money and be part of her close team, he'd have to learn, wouldn't he.

This was beyond a dog's dinner. She couldn't think properly. On the one hand, her mind was fudged from lack of sleep, from the shock of seeing Bob, and on the other, she needed to work out the best course of action here.

Before the sun reared its big ball of a head.

The police car—would it still be burning? If it wasn't, was it too hot for her clean-up crew to move? Ideally, to stop the police sniffing around, she needed to get rid of it. She had a scrappy on her books who disposed of vehicles, crunching them up into compacted squares, so that wasn't a problem. He was used to being woken up in the middle of the night with a delivery, asking no questions.

She had to act on this now so sent a message to her crew. The light in the hallway snapping on and Mam coming out of the house, fully dressed, meant she'd gone in the kitchen at the back and closed the door, hence the previous darkness. She'd probably been sitting at the island with a whiskey, steadying her nerves not only after shooting Zhang Wei and their disposal of two bodies, but also setting fire to a fucking police car. While Cassie had been torturing Jason, Mam had been doing her own kind of illegal deed.

Cassie walked to the door and gestured for Mam and Lou to go inside. Her phone bleeped again, and while the older women went down the hallway, Cassie checked her screen.

Crew One: *On our way.*

Cassie: *Be quick. Be careful.*

Crew One: *We always are.*

She locked up and joined Mam and Lou in the kitchen. Lou sat at the island, spine straight, a creepy smile in place. Mam had coffee on the go. Cassie sat opposite Lou, able to take her in properly now the light was on. The farmer's wife had a mental-case gleam in her eyes, and she twitched, most likely manic with the excitement of what she'd done, what was happening now. Cassie understood that feeling well—hadn't she got some perverse pleasure from hurting people? Especially Jason, the little bastard, trying to take the Barrington off her. Cutting Karen's stomach up had given Cassie a massive rush, too, another turncoat who'd planned to rule the patch.

Dad had warned her this might happen, but *two* people doing it? Were there others who hated her style of command and planned to snatch the estate from her? Why did they think they had the right?

"We'll have a coffee while we make plans," she said, "then we'll go to the factory. The crew are sorting the police car." She gave Lou a dirty look. "Mam, you'll deal with Bob and Marlene—you'll also need to sort the brains Lou put in a carrier bag. Once we're finished, I'll go to the squat to burn the bag and Bob's clothes."

"This is so exciting" Lou said.

You bloody weirdo.

Mam shivered, pausing with her hand on a mug, and Cassie took it that her mother thought Lou was disturbed, too.

No more disturbed than me putting the flaps of Karen's stomach skin in my pocket.

Cassie eyed the nutter. "Lou, me and you will clean up the ground behind the factory and also scrub your boot and the tyres—there's no way I can get the valet on it unless you can cover your arse with Joe. He'll wonder where your car is if I

24

drop you off." She glanced at the clock on the wall. "Speaking of Joe. What time does he get up?"

"Five. Today he's just got to clean out the pigs."

"What if he rolls over in bed and finds you're not there?" Mam brought the drinks over and sat.

Lou shrugged. "I've gone for drives during the night before. He knows I get restless."

Fine.

"Okay, what are your plans going forward? How many coppers are you going to 'farm'?" It had given Cassie the willies when Lou had announced she was now The Piggy Farmer, intent on farming all the coppers out of the area, the ones who'd failed her daughter. That had to be a large number. The amount of police involved in a missing child case/murder ran into the hundreds, surely.

No way can we kill all of them.

"Four main ones. There were five, but one died already. Don't worry, I don't plan to bump off the whole force." Lou laughed, picked up her coffee, and blew on it. She sipped, taking her time about it an' all. "Bob was the first one, although originally he was last on my shit list, so there are three more."

"Why Bob?" Cassie watched the steam rising from her cup and wished she was in the office filling in the coded ledger, not sitting here with some deranged woman.

"Because he did door-to-door enquiries and didn't go inside The Mechanic's house—in *anyone's* house on his designated route. All the other uniforms went inside properties, but Bob? He was pals with The Mechanic, so of *course* he'd bloody well ignore his orders on that score. If he'd gone in, had a look around, he'd have found

26

my Jess locked in that upstairs office. Alive."
Tears glistened in her eyes, eyes that no longer
had the mad gleam but shadows of sadness. "I
listen to gossip whenever I'm away from the
farm, and everyone admitted he'd just spoken to
them at their doors. He let my little girl down."

Cassie swallowed the lump in her throat. She
just about remembered playing with Jess, but
those memories were hazy. Who could recall
everything from when they were three? "What
about the other pigs? Who are they?"

Lou's face scrunched in distaste. "DCI Robin
Gorley, DC Simon Knight, and DS Lisa
Codderidge. They led the investigation, and none
of them thought to check Bob's route and what
he'd done on it. Or hadn't done."

Cassie played devil's advocate. "He might
have lied on his reports, said he'd entered homes,
so it wouldn't be their fault."

Lou didn't appear to want to listen to that, wafting her hand about in dismissal. "Whatever, they didn't find Jess, and they're responsible for her death as much as Vance bastard Johnson. I want justice, and while Vance is now dead, it's not enough anymore."

Will it ever be enough? Will she ever stop searching for retribution? "How do you propose to kill the rest?"

Lou appeared smug. "I know where they go when they're not at work. I've kept my ears and eyes open for a long while. Over twenty bloody years, Cass. You can think up a lot of revenge during that time. The DCI's retired now. He likes his allotment, even goes there in this weather. Sits in his shed for hours on end instead of growing stuff. The DI and DS are having a fling, have been for yonks—they meet up at The Lion's Head then shag behind it. You know the one, on the Moor estate. I've followed them, seen it with my own eyes."

The Moor estate. Where Zhang Wei opened The Golden Dragon. "Was it just by chance you were driving earlier and saw Bob then, or did you already know his night shift routine if you've been following these people?"

"He always drove past the farm at the same time of night, like he had a route he stuck by. I stare out of the window a lot when I have insomnia. I just happened to go after him earlier. Couldn't sleep again." Lou rubbed her forehead. "I was fired up from feeding the pigs."

That weird gleam came back.

Cassie suppressed a shudder. "So, you didn't answer my question. How do you plan to kill the coppers?" She turned to Mam. "I take it you're helping."

Mam nodded. "We've discussed it, yes, but not to any great degree."

Cassie sighed. "Then we need to plan. Properly. Four coppers going missing is going to create a stir. We act fast, get them all done as quickly as we can. Then maybe we can return to some form of normality."

It was a nice thought, but somehow, Cassie knew that wasn't going to happen. Running the Barrington meant she had to be on her toes at all times, so nowt was ever normal. There was always someone in the shadows, waiting to cause trouble.

Not for the first time, she cursed her father's dodgy heart. She wouldn't be surprised if hers went the same way, what with all the stress.

Chapter Two

The Barrington Life – Your Weekly

JESS WILSON'S FUNERAL

Karen Scholes – All Things Crime in our Time
Sharon Barnett – Chief Editor

FRIDAY EVENING EDITION. JULY 11TH 1997

As many of you know, our lovely little Jessica Wilson was laid to rest, the police finally releasing her body to her parents. What a turnout. Thanks to everyone who came to show Joe and Lou their support – and thank you for doing what they wanted by buying your children something nice rather than spending it on flowers.

What I came to realise as I stood in that church and stared at that tiny coffin was: life is never guaranteed. We gad about thinking we have all the time in the world, don't we, making plans for the future, when that very future isn't always there waiting for us. Jess was supposed to grow up and fall in love, marry, and have kids. Instead… Well, we all know what happened. Tragic.

No bones about it, the police are useless. I'm not sorry for saying that either. I mean, come on, what were they doing, picking their noses? That child should never have been snatched, never have been held against her will, and never, ever should she have been dumped by The Beast on Sculptor's Field. What kind of society do we live in for that to happen? Makes me sick.

The second kidnapper who was in the back of the van is still at large. We need to remain vigilant, watch our kiddies, in case whoever that was decides to do it again. Hold your child's hand a bit tighter. Don't let the smaller ones play outside by themselves. If it takes sitting on your doorstep while they kick a football in the road or whatever, that's what you have to do. They're precious, our kids, and if I find out someone's ignored these rules, I'll be letting Lenny know. He'll deal with you.

Anyroad, I got carried away there. Once again, thank you for going to the funeral. Big hugs to Sharon for buying the balloons with Jess' name on them. When we all let them go, I got massive goosebumps and hoped Jess could see them from Heaven. She's an angel now, forever in our hearts.

Lou sighed and pushed The Barrington Life *leaflet across the kitchen table. It had arrived an hour ago,*

Karen Scholes probably rushing home to write it. Sometimes, that woman was macabre the way she jumped on anyone's misfortune and spread it around the Barrington. All right, Lenny had probably told her to do it, but still, some things could be left alone, couldn't they? At least until tomorrow. It wasn't that Lou didn't want Jess in the forefront of people's minds, she did, just not this minute.

She was drained from the funeral, absolutely washed out having to speak to so many people, accepting their condolences, lying and saying she'd be okay when she fucking well wouldn't. She'd never be okay again. It had seemed like her body didn't belong to her anymore, going through the motions, shaking hands, allowing people to hug her, and all the while, her soul had screamed: "Stop! Make this stop! Please, just leave me be."

While she was grateful they'd come, taking the time out of their lives to attend, she wished she'd limited it to family and close friends. Instead, it seemed all of the Barrington had turned up, hundreds coming together as a community to mourn the heart-breaking loss of her child, some having to remain outside the church. Or, as she'd bitterly contemplated when the crowd was twenty-deep around the hole in the ground, they'd come for the excitement, something to bring drama to an otherwise shite day, and then had a reason to get bladdered in The Donny from the free bar Lenny had provided, not to mention the gorgeous spread, a buffet he'd paid some company to make. There had even been a cake made by Nicola in The Shoppe Pudding, little pink wellies on top, anchors for a fondant girl with curly blonde hair and a pretty ballerina dress.

A sweet Jess, as she'd been while alive.

Lou had taken it, wrapped it in a napkin, and once home, she'd placed it in a box and hid it at the back of a kitchen cupboard. One day it would crack, become distorted, a memory ruined by time, and she'd mourn that fondant girl along with the real thing.

No one would mourn more than her, she was sure of that. She was still in a state of shock, living in a surreal world where her daughter was gone but her heart refused to accept it. To get through since the discovery of the body, she'd pretended Jess was staying with family, on an extended holiday down south. Cornwall, playing in the sand, building castles. She'd have a pink bucket—Jess loved pink—and a pink spade, and she'd have a strawberry ice cream in a cone. She'd giggle when the sea whooshed up to bite her tiny toes, screeching as it chased her up the beach.

I'll never hear that giggle again except in my head.

Joe had gone to bed, dog-tired from grief, from the enormity of standing there while such an obscenely small casket had been lowered into a just as obscenely small hole, so Lou had some time to herself now, precious time away from someone worrying over her. She got up and wandered upstairs to Jess' room, quiet, so Joe didn't hear her in his sleep and wake, asking if she was okay.

Everything was exactly as it should be in this toddler's paradise, and every night since the kidnap, Lou had closed the curtains and switched on the lamp. Every morning she did the opposite, letting in the light of day, telling herself Jess would be back soon, sand between her toes, in her sandals, and the bottom of her suitcase.

It had helped her get through.

Two items of Jess' had been returned despite the police saying they'd be needed as evidence. Lenny had worked his magic, telling a high-up pig in his pocket that the man who'd killed Jess would be quietly dealt with, so why hold on to those possessions? Somehow—rules broken, Lou had no doubt of that—she'd received the pink wellies and the transparent rainbow coat.

The post-mortem had revealed strangulation, the marks of hands around her dainty throat emerging an hour or so after Karen Scholes had found the body on Sculptor's Field, the broken hyoid bone, the tiny red spots around her eyes—all of it evidence that someone had throttled her child.

Who could do such a thing?

Lou sat on the bed with its ballerina duvet and smoothed her hand over the pillow. One of Jess' hairs snagged on the diamond of her engagement ring, and Lou held it up to the light from the lamp, crying at the way that hair glimmered. It had always glimmered, but now the rest of it was beneath the ground in a box, ready to rot. Eventually, her baby would have bugs eating her eyes and crawling in her mouth and—

She imagined this sort of thing daily, tormenting herself. Was it any wonder she'd gone slightly mad? Who in their right mind could cope with such images and the hurt they produced? But she couldn't help it;

seemed she wanted to feel the pain as penance for not being at the factory when Jess had been stolen. If she'd been there, the man wouldn't have taken her. Lou would've fought to snatch her from his arms.

Correction: the man wouldn't have got near her in the first place, as Lou always, always held her hand and kept her close.

Did she blame Joe? A little—how could she not? With grief, you had to blame someone, didn't you, had to have one or two people you held accountable. He should have been holding her hand. He should have fought harder. But he had tried, and she wasn't so mental and twisted that she couldn't see how such situations spiralled out of control. Everyone who'd been there had told her he'd turned into a lion, defending his cub, and it had happened so fast he hadn't been able to stop it.

Then there was the gun pointed his way.

Ninety-five percent of her didn't hold him responsible, but the other five... She'd have to work hard not to let her feelings show, keep them tucked away inside, find someone else to settle her blame on. Joe was broken, and he carried enough guilt as it was.

What about the police?

She allowed scenarios to enter her mind, watching them as film snippets: her spying on the coppers involved; planning how to waylay them without being seen; killing them for their part in this. Yes, that would keep her going throughout the coming years. She'd have a focus, even if she didn't follow through.

She couldn't let herself remain on that train of thought and told herself such things would never happen. No, she'd never kill a police officer—she'd killed someone with Doreen Prince once, and that was enough for her. And Jess would never have bugs crawling all over her, not in Lou's mind. She'd remain preserved in the coffin, as perfect in death as she'd been in life.

And anyroad, she was in Cornwall, wasn't she, living down there.

It was better to tell herself that.

Chapter Three

Jason was dreaming. Or, more to the point, having a nightmare. Odd how you knew it was a dream, yet you were asleep and should know no such thing. Pain soared in his leg, and if he wasn't mistaken, it was nailed to the floor. He wasn't sure how he knew that, but dreams had a way about them where they just *told* you stuff, didn't they, gave you knowledge. There you were, in whatever situation—he was usually fighting his dad and killing him, saving Mam from the arsehole—all the information *there*.

It was the agony that was the biggest clue regarding the nail, and the constant *feel* of it; if he moved his leg even a millimetre, the solid spike made itself known, as did the pain, the heat, the utter wretchedness, the broken bone where the nail had pierced through it.

He urged himself to wake up—in his bed, not the squat where he guessed his subconscious mind had placed him—but the struggle was too much. He was tired, and alcohol still floated through his body. Was that part of the dream or reality? Had he been on a bender? The remnants of Jack Daniel's clung to his furry tongue, so that was a possibility, but the taste of old blood didn't make sense.

Alcohol-induced nightmares were a right old wanker.

A noise. Someone shuffling? It sounded like shoes shushing over carpet.

"Ah, you're coming round then. Do you need some painkillers?" A pause. "If you give me any bother, Cassie says I have to knock you back out, just so you know. Punch you, like."

Jason frowned, and the action hurt his sore face. It was on fire, tight with what he could only assume was dried blood. The smell of it was strong, the copper pennies of childhood inside a piggy bank.

And…hang on, why the fuck was Jimmy Lews talking to him?

Jason opened his eyes—or he thought he did. They seemed already open, scratchy and dry, and they'd just rolled down from on high, as though he didn't have any eyelids. He breathed in through his nose, and more air than usual entered—one nostril was bigger than the other?

A gauzy Jimmy bent over him, peering right into Jason's face. Jesus Christ, that acne of his… It was a hair's breadth away, livid, some spots with yellow pus on the verge of breaking through the surface.

You'd think he'd make a visit to Superdrug, wouldn't you, get some cream.

"Gerraway," Jason mumbled, his bottom lip heavy. He tried to bat Jimmy off, but his hands were tied behind his back. Was this situation showing him what it was like to be held captive at the squat? Did a small part of him feel guilty over what he'd done to people here and it was manifesting in a dream?

No, he never felt guilty, so what was this all about?

"Are you going to behave?" Jimmy eased back, and he grew smaller, indistinct, a dark fuzzy shadow surrounded by yellow light, too yellow to just be the bare bulb dangling above his head. "Because I don't want to hit you. Don't forget I've got a gun an' all. I'll use it, but it doesn't mean I'll get any joy from it."

Jason scrabbled to work this out. Jimmy with a gun didn't sound right. The pimply fuckface was someone Lenny had used as a message runner in the past, but he wasn't the sort to have a weapon. Where would he have got it from? It didn't make sense.

Shit, did he steal mine?

"Gun?" Jason managed to grind out. God, his bottom lip hurt, throbbed. It was thick, swollen, and taut in one section, as if something held it together. Invisible pliers.

Jimmy's shadow nodded, the head moving in stuttered slow motion. "Yeah. What's up with you? Don't you remember?"

Remember what?

Jason hated not being in control, and this dream was doing his bloody nut in. Fresh pain speared his leg, joining the relentless ache-burn, and he moaned, too tired to scream. His throat was sore anyroad, as though he'd already screeched for England or it was parched from lack of water, and his energy level was too low— he needed to keep what he had to think, and even that was difficult.

"Cazzee…?" he said and detested how that word had come out.

"You were a right prat messing with her." Jimmy loomed back into view, one of his spots about to erupt far too close for comfort. "Only a prick would try to take the patch off her."

Prick. Jimmy had called him a prick.

Rage festered in Jason's gut, more so because he didn't have it in him to react to the slur, one his waste-of-space father had always called him. The dream-nightmare was doing a number on him, preventing him from acting as he usually would, and he didn't like it. If he could get his hands free, stand, he'd beat the shit out of Jimmy.

"Pizz…off." He hovered on the brink of going deeper under or waking up. Which one needed more effort? Waking. It would be so easy to let himself drift, and he longed for oblivion to take him.

"Piss off?" Jimmy moved away again. "I can't do that. Cassie wouldn't like it. You know, you wouldn't be here if you'd done as you were told, accepted her as the boss. I can't believe you thought you'd get away with it."

Jason focused better, forcing himself to see clearly, although his eyeballs had a strained feel to them. Had they bugged out at some point? He ignored the pain in his leg, which had been a steady throb lanced with spiky hurt so far, and concentrated. Ahead, an old bookcase. To the left, a window with the blackout blind drawn. Yellow wallpaper peeling from the top— so *that* was why the light was this weird mustard colour, it had reflected off the walls. A scabby carpet, beige that had once been dove-grey—he knew that as a certainty. And the smell… Dried piss, mould, and lavender.

It was all so familiar yet foreign at the same time—foreign because he didn't understand why he was here, how he'd got here, or whether it was real or not. Yes, he was definitely in the squat, the house the old lady had left to Lenny as payment for whatever he'd done to help her out. The place where Jason had tortured many, loving the power.

How frustrating not to have any now. Maybe *that* was what the dream was teaching him. To give up his need to control the Barrington. Or was it saying that despite what he thought, he'd never have control, even if he took over running it for Cassie? She'd always be the boss, no matter what.

Jimmy stood by the open doorway, beside the bookcase, and became clearer. With that clarity, more pain seared Jason's wrecked shin bone and infiltrated the surrounding muscles, a seeping heat that combined with a swelling sensation, his skin stretching, like it would rip any second.

He imagined a balloon popping. Tested out his dream state and moved his leg.

And was sucked under in a maelstrom of agony, Jimmy and the scabby living room disappearing, sending Jason into what he could only imagine were the depths of Hell, where flames devoured his leg, intent on suffocating him with the intensity.

Jimmy relaxed, thankful Jason had blacked out again, although it was a bit bloody weird how his eyes had gone upwards, showing only the whites threaded with red veins. At least Jason hadn't caused a problem; Jimmy wouldn't have to punch him now. One, he wasn't into violence, and seeing Cassie mete it out had churned his sensitive stomach, and two, his knuckles would come into contact with Jason's mashed-up face. It'd be like thumping minced beef.

Cassie had wrecked it with her new weapon, the whip with barbed wire wrapped around it. Jimmy had heard of it via *The Barrington Life*, but to actually see it being used… Barbs had munched on Jason's cheeks, ripping his skin, taking his eyelids and one eyebrow off, slicing through his bottom lip, cutting off a chunk of one nostril. Cassie had sewn it up, that lip—*fucking hell!*—acting like it was the most natural thing in the world to be doing that on a freezing February night.

Like she'd enjoyed it.

Jimmy would never get on her bad side.

Christ, this was a job and a half, wasn't it, something he never thought he'd do. Babysitting a man pinned to the floor by an eight-inch nail, Jason Shepherd at that, Cassie Grafton's right hand. Earlier, in The Donny, Jimmy had got Jason drunk during a lock-in and recorded a confession about taking over the patch. While Jimmy had known Cassie would go mad once she heard it, he hadn't thought she'd go *this* mad.

Then again, he should have expected it. She'd made it clear she wasn't going to take shit from anyone, and she'd proved that by including the one man she should have trusted the most, the one who was meant to have her back. Why did Jason think it was a good idea to take over the patch when he knew Cassie was a mental case? He must have seen her in action plenty of times since she'd stepped in for Lenny, and prior to that even, with Lenny taking a load off for six months before he'd died. On what planet was it wise to cross her?

None in this universe.

Jimmy stared at Jason. He *might* feel a bit sorry for him, to be honest. Jason had got too big for his fancy shoes, so much so they'd given him symbolic blisters, and maybe this punishment would teach him to get back in his place and forget the idea of ruling. Jimmy didn't reckon he would, though, not really. Jason was intent on running the patch, and a shattered shin bone and fucked-up mush wouldn't stop him.

Only death would.

"Don't fucking think about that," Jimmy warned himself.

Bloody hell, being here was driving him so crackers he was talking to himself. Someone had dropped bags of food and a telly off earlier, a bloke in black clothes, great stomping boots with thick soles, and a balaclava. The latter had shit Jimmy up, the eyes such a piercing green he'd know them if he saw them again. He had no clue who they belonged to and didn't really need to. The least he was aware of the better. He'd just do as he was told and ask no questions. Unsettling, though, that whoever it had been knew who *he* was now.

"Maybe he had contact lenses in."

Unable to stand it any longer, the pacing, the boredom—even hooking the telly up didn't appeal—he took his personal phone out to tap in a message on WhatsApp to Shirl, his girlfriend. He'd already phoned to give her the gist of things but needed the contact for a sense of normality in this utter insanity, despite the time of night—or morning, as it happened. He didn't think she'd be sleeping anyroad, not with the news he'd told her.

How their lives had changed. One minute they'd both had mundane jobs, eking their wages out, minding their own business, and the next, Cassie had come round and offered them another kind of job, five hundred quid a week each, to listen, be her 'ears'.

Amongst other stuff.

Stuff like this task now, looking after a man who'd most likely be dead come the light of day. Jason's leg had bled so much, a large patch of red had soaked into the manky carpet. If he didn't die from the loss, he'd die another way.

And Cassie would be the murderer, because *Jimmy* didn't fancy using the gun.

He sighed and got hold of Shirl.

Jimmy: *I've been thinking. I don't want you doing your shifts with You Know Who. It's not something I want you involved in.*

Shirl: *Won't C be upset about that? We can't afford to piss her off, Jim.*

Jimmy: *I'll talk to her. Say you're ill and I'll do all the stints. Sleep on the floor or whatever. It's not nice here. I can't even cope with it, so you?*

Shirl: *I have to be honest, I don't want to watch him. Or watch her when she comes back, doing what you said she did. I knew there was something off about her when we were at school together. She always gave me the creeps. Always scared me.*

Jimmy: *Nah, it was the fact she's Lenny's daughter that scared you. She's nice enough underneath it all, and I get why she's doing this, even if it's loony. Her old man worked hard, and she's not going to let someone like Jason whip it away from her. But this place, it's shite. He woke up but has gone back to sleep. It's like he didn't know where he was or why he's here.*

Shirl: *What do you think she's going to do with him?*

Jimmy: *I don't even want to go there.*

Shirl: *Fucking hell.*

Jimmy: *I know. Listen, try to get some sleep. I'll sort things with C. We'll say you've come down with the flu or whatever. She's not a complete monster, she won't expect you to work if you're ill. Just stay in the flat until this is over, so it looks like you're holed up in bed.*

Shirl: *Okay. Will you be all right?*

Jimmy: *Yeah. Just got to hope I'm not here too long. I don't think he's going to last. It's the blood, see. He's still got booze in him, so when that wears off…*

Shirl: *That leg's going to hurt.*

Jimmy: *Tell me about it. Night.*

Shirl: *Night xxx*

Jimmy felt better now. Shirl having to use a gun on Jason didn't sit well, even just threatening him with it, not for the amount of money Cassie had paid. Killing was about twenty-five grand in his book, not the five she'd handed over for babysitting—*and* that had to be split between him and Shirl. No, five for watching this prat he could handle, but murder? He'd want a hell of a lot more, despite there being no risk because Cassie would smooth everything over.

The thing was, did he have the balls to say that to a Grafton? *Look, love, I need another twenty if you want me to shoot him, else I'm off.*

He laughed at the stupidity of it.

Antsy, needing a breather before he wound himself up further, he checked Jason and, satisfied the bloke would be out of it for a while, he turned the living room light off and left the squat to stand outside and smoke.

It was hard to believe such bad things happened when presented with a white blanket of snow that reeked of childhood and going outside to play in it, cheeks cold, the tip of his nose chill-bitten. The air had a muffled quality, as though the white stuff suffocated any sounds, and there he stood, in the footprints of Balaclava Man on the front step, the door pulled to behind him, lighting up and inhaling, the frosty air going down along with the warm smoke.

He turned to his left, and a speck of orange-yellow in the distance caught his eye. A fire? It winked out, and blackness took its place. Maybe he'd imagined it; he was tired after all. He shrugged and finished his ciggie for five minutes or so, nipped back in to check Jason, made a coffee in one of the to-go cups Balaclava had brought, then came back out again, sparking up another fag.

The rumble of car engines sabotaged the silence, and he turned to his left once more. Headlights cracked slices into the night, one set low, the other high, as if belonging to a car and a lorry. They chuntered past and, as the snow lent extra light, he made out a small dark hatchback and a tow truck behind, a burnt-out vehicle on the back. So he *had* seen a fire. God, had there been an accident down the way a bit, the car blowing up after a crash? Would the police come along any second, spot him, and ask what he was doing here?

Jimmy shivered from the cold and dipped his head, anxious in case the drivers copped sight of him. The last thing Cassie wanted was people getting interested in the squat, a place that was supposedly empty, of no use to anyone. But if he dashed indoors now, it'd look well weird, bringing more attention.

That shiver was also from fear. He'd fucked up by coming out here, taken a risk. He'd forgotten to switch the living room light off again when he'd checked Jason, and it seeped into the hallway, probably turning him into a highly visible silhouette, seeing as he hadn't shut the door behind him this time.

Shite. Should he tell Cassie or keep that to himself? Would she be angrier if she found out someone had seen him and he hadn't said, than she would if he confessed straight away?

You said you didn't want to get on her bad side…

The vehicles drove towards the Barrington, the taillights of the recovery lorry creepy rectangular eyes, glowing red, the Devil's irises. That shiver came back, and Jimmy stepped inside, knowing what he had to do, no matter the consequences. He locked up, entered the living room, and closed the door.

Jimmy: *I went outside for a fag. Might have been seen by someone in a car and a recovery lorry.*

Cassie: *Don't worry about it. They're my people. Too busy atm. Talk soon. [smile emoji]*

Jimmy's relief left him weak. That could have gone the other way if those drivers weren't something to do with her. Luck seemed to be on his side, and that creature called Curiosity reared its head.

Why had a car been set alight, and what did it have to do with Cassie?

Chapter Four

Lou stood at the back door of the farmhouse as if Cassie's knock had woken her. She'd nipped in to get her tartan blanket and wrapped it around herself, playing the role they'd planned.

"What's the matter?" she said, sounding worried. Loud.

Oh, she's good at this.

"Sorry to bother you again so soon, but we need to feed the pigs." Cassie said that in case Joe had woken up and listened in.

This had to seem authentic. Lou was insistent he couldn't know what she'd been up to—or what she'd be *getting* up to in the future. She'd said something in Mam's kitchen, regarding having to keep another secret about murder, and she couldn't handle Joe knowing who she'd really been before they'd started seeing one another. Mam had given Lou a look: *Don't say a word.*

So she was in on whatever had gone down, and Cassie was to remain in the dark, was that it?

Maybe it's better I don't know all the details.

Lou sniffed. "Hang on, let me just get Joe. He was asleep the last time I looked in on him."

She disappeared inside, and Cassie turned to Mam, who stood beside her, bundled into a padded black parka, her hands stuffed into the pockets. Thick flakes of snow flurried down, dancing in front of her face, one landing on her cheek and dissolving.

Mam had fed Bob's body into Marlene, Cassie helping her to lift him, then Cassie and Lou had cleaned the mess out the back of the factory, scraping the bloodied snow up where the brain and blood had spattered. Together, they'd washed the tyres, dug up blood from the compacted snow tracks Lou had made when driving off. Once Bob was minced and Marlene cleaned, they'd hauled the plastic box containing his remains onto the trolley and transferred it to Cassie's boot.

They just had to hope Joe hadn't roused while Lou had been absent, off killing a bloody copper, for fuck's sake. He hadn't phoned or texted her, so maybe he was still dead to the world, and anyroad, Lou would use that excuse of going for a drive, insomnia sending her out into the white night. However, if he *had* woken up, Cassie wasn't in the right frame of mind for any questions being aired while she was there. Lou would have to deal with them by herself behind closed doors. Yes, Cassie and Mam were helping her to become The Piggy Farmer, but that didn't mean they had to do so with every aspect.

No, Lou had to cover her own arse with her husband. Cassie would only step in if it was absolutely necessary, if it had the potential to bring hassle to her or Mam.

"I'm so knackered," she whispered, her eyes gritty, bones weary. Her bed was calling, but she wasn't likely to see it much before five a.m. at this rate. She might not even bother going to bed at all.

Mam chuckled. "It gets you like that, killing. I remember how I used to feel as though I'd been run over once the adrenaline wore off. A murder hangover."

Cassie held her breath for a moment so she didn't respond like a spoilt brat—Mam being involved in murder wasn't something she'd known about until the last few hours, but they'd discussed it, and there wasn't any sense in bringing it up again. The past was the past, and Cassie had more than enough in the now to deal with without raking up old stories and kept secrets, no matter how much it rankled.

She ploughed on with the news she hadn't told Mam yet, what with Lou being at their house earlier, Bob's death interrupting the flow. "Jason's in the squat, pinned to the floor by a long nail. I used my weapon on him. He doesn't have any eyelids." It was so awful said out loud, and she was well aware of how detached she sounded. A coping mechanism?

Mam's laugh was ominous and had a creepy cadence to it, like she relished the image that had probably perked up in her head, Jason unable to move, blood everywhere, his smug face wrecked. "No more than he deserves—he knows what you're like and was stupid to think he'd be immune to any punishment. That's his ego again, that is. So, you properly cottoned on in the end then, agreed with me. I knew he was dodgy. Didn't I *say* he was right from the night your father died? I told you I wanted it on record how I felt."

Cassie kept her voice low. "All right, no need to rub it in." She pushed on so that train of conversation didn't continue. "Jimmy recorded him in The Donny for me. Jason was definitely trying to take over the patch."

"What a sly little bastard. What are your plans for him?" Mam's cloud of breath floated past the open back door. "You know what I'd opt for."

Cassie hugged herself for warmth. "Well, he can't live, can he. Not after this."

"Exactly my thought."

Footsteps prevented them from discussing it further. Joe appeared, his cheek red from being pressed to a pillow. He'd dressed hastily by the look of him, his shirt done up wonky, the collar sitting wrong, higher on one side than the other, his canvas-type trousers open at the button. He fixed that and came towards them, socked feet whispering on the lino then deadening as he stepped onto the bristly mat.

"Another one?" He shook his head. "I don't even want to know."

"No, you don't." Cassie smiled. "So, shall we get on with it then?"

"I'll need to get my wellies on."

Joe ambled to the right of the mudroom, scratching the back of his head, and Lou came outside, her blanket wrapped even tighter around her.

Cassie wondered why Lou had insisted on waking him. Perhaps it was to secure her alibi in his eyes, her earlier mention coming into play of him not needing to know her secrets, that she'd been outside while he'd slept on, oblivious. Or maybe he'd said he should be present every time the pigs got an extra feed. Or Lou, although hiding the fact she'd killed a copper from him, and God knew who else, didn't like to lie to him by letting Cassie and Mam into the barn without his knowledge. It was, after all, his farm. Whatever, the sooner they dumped Bob's remains the better. Mam would return to the factory to wash out the plastic tub—she'd brought her own car—and Cassie had to nip to the squat to burn Bob's clothes.

It didn't take long to dispose of Mr Plod, the pigs gorging on the clumps of flesh, and afterwards, Lou disappeared into the farmhouse, Joe remaining on the doorstep.

"Fair warning, I'll be bringing Jason here at some point." Cassie stamped her feet to chase the chill off. "Might be tomorrow night, might be the one after, depending on how long I want to string things out. There's shit I need him to admit first."

"Jason?" His eyebrows arched.

"Yes."

"Right. I don't have to say I'll be keeping that to myself."

"I know, Joe. Thanks, and sorry for getting you up again."

They left him, Mam driving towards the factory, Cassie going the other way. Out of curiosity, she sailed past the squat to the location of the previously burning car, satisfied her cleaners had come and gone, even going so far as to rake snow over the melted patch where the heat had got to it. No one would know owt had ever happened, what with more snow falling, fat flakes that settled on her hair.

She brushed them off and got back in the car, threw Bob's phone battery into the bushes on the way, and arrived at the squat inside a couple of minutes. She messaged Jimmy to warn him she was there—so he didn't shit himself or whatever—and studied the house to ensure no light seeped around the blinds. To anyone passing, it would appear as desolate as always.

Her phone blipped.

Jimmy: *Okay. I'm in the kitchen.*

The carrier bag of Bob's clothes in hand, she let herself in, locked up, and poked her head into the living room. Jason was obviously where she'd left him—it wasn't like he could sodding move, was it. The bloodstain beneath his leg had got bigger since she was last here, as to be expected, and his face had dried out a bit, presenting him as a burn victim, all that raw flesh with a hardening crust. His lower lip had ballooned even more, especially around the tight stiches, giving the top-of-a-love-heart vibe. The whites of his eyes told her he was out of it, the faintest bottom curves of his irises visible at the top. Red veins crawled up to them, lightning strikes produced by pressure, and her monster smiled at her handiwork, pleased she'd had it in her to inflict such pain.

How *dare* he want to swoop in and take what her father had spent so many years building up.

All that hard work, handed to Jason on a gold plate? Not fucking likely.

She walked down the hallway into the kitchen. Jimmy poured boiled water into two cups. He looked tired and jumpy.

"All right?" She moved to the furnace and opened the door. Welcome heat blasted out, the force of it waving her hair.

"Bored, to be honest," Jimmy said. "There's nowt like being in your own home, is there."

Cassie knew that feeling. While she'd loved staying at Mam's, she'd missed her little flat. It may be attached to the house, but it still felt separate. Hers. "It does get like that, yes."

She checked over her shoulder to ensure Jimmy wasn't watching—he was adding milk to the cups—then whipped Bob's uniform and hat out of the bag, shoving them into the furnace.

Next went his shoes, shiny black ones, treading the beat no more, and his work phone, his ID.

She flung the carrier inside and snapped the door closed. "Owt to report other than the breakdown lorry incident?" She joined Jimmy at the worktop.

He blushed. "I'm right sorry about that. I didn't expect anyone to come along, not at that time."

"You're entitled to fresh air, you know, just go out the back in future. It's only miles of fields that way, no roads."

"Okay." He bit his lip. "I saw a fire. It was far away, like."

"Yes, we needed to torch a vehicle. Nowt to worry about. It's the usual thing. Had to get rid of it."

She wasn't going to elaborate, tell the truth. He could think what he wanted, wondering why she hadn't used the car-crusher bloke straight away, why it even needed torching. No doubt Bob's disappearance would make the local news, *and* the fact his patrol car was missing, and Jimmy would put two and two together.

Not a lot she could do about that. Nor could she do owt about any trackers on the police car. She assumed there was some way Control knew where the officers were. That meant, if the tracker had stopped working in the fire, the last location would still be known.

Shit. She'd have to get Mam to have a word with a new pig-in-their-pocket copper, one high up enough to steer nosy officers away from the squat. She quickly sent her a message to deal with that.

Jimmy drew her out of her head. "Shirl's got hold of me. She's got the flu, so if it's all right with you, I'll do the babysitting on my own."

"Fine, so long as one of you is here. There's a blow-up bed in the cupboard under the stairs, a foot pump, and a few blankets, a pillow. You can doss down in the living room."

"Cheers." He stirred the drinks then pushed a chipped mug across the worktop towards her. "He woke up. Jason. Didn't seem to know what was going on."

"I don't suppose he did, considering the pain he's in. The dickhead's probably delirious."

"Will he be here for long?" Jimmy sipped some coffee.

Cassie picked hers up and wrapped her hands around it to warm her cold fingers. "Is that you asking out of compassion for him? Or is it so you know how long you'll be here?"

"The last one."

"Good. Feeling sorry for him isn't a great idea. He's a snake, remember that. The shit he's been up to behind my back…" She drank, pushing thoughts of Nathan Abbott out of her head, someone she'd killed. "But to answer the question, I don't know. I've got something else to deal with, unfortunately, so Jason will have to remain here until I'm done. That could be a couple of days. I'll try to nip back and finish him off before that, though."

Jimmy flinched.

"What?" she said. "You know what I do."

He shrugged. "Yeah, but seeing it…"

She sighed. Honestly, she was too tired to deal with Jimmy having a wobble. "Have you got a problem doing this job? If you do, say so now."

He appeared to struggle with the answer. Then, "Nah. I'll do it. I said I would, and I won't go back on a promise."

Cassie stared over at the furnace, the flames going mental, burning the evidence. "Glad to hear it. I'm using you because I don't want others knowing what's going on, so asking someone else to cover for you, no ta. His mother, Gina… I don't want her interfering. I'll tell her afterwards, of course, let her know if she kicks up a fuss she'll get the same treatment, but if she knows he's alive and being kept somewhere, she may well go to the police, and that wouldn't be wise."

Jimmy swallowed, and it wasn't coffee. "I'm not saying this in a bad way, just curious, because I need to know. How do you sleep at night?" He laughed nervously. "Asking for a friend."

The poor bastard. He must have a feeling he'd struggle on that front. To be fair, he had seen some horrific shit, and it was likely fucking with his mind. She'd been there, where she'd seen it all over again later on, playing out inside her head even while she was awake.

"You learn to compartmentalise." She wasn't about to tell him the monster inside her enjoyed it to a certain degree, that part of her looked forward to hurting people. That was for her and her alone to know, or maybe Mam. "It's what was handed down to me, a legacy if you like. The murder, the torture, the running of the patch, doing things people should never do, but I promised my dad I would, so there you go. Like you, I don't break promises if I can help it. Listen, I won't ask you to do owt like this again if you don't want me to, if you're uncomfortable with it. You were originally meant to be my grass, weren't you, it's just that things happened, escalated."

"Hmm, I get it, no worries on that score. And I'll get used to it if you have plans for me. Like, if you need me for owt else that's nasty."

Had he said that because he thought he had no choice, even though she'd basically said he did? Didn't he trust her?

"I'm not going to *make* you do stuff, Jim, but if you want to do it to earn extra, I won't say no."

He shifted from foot to foot. "I'm not being rude but—"

"People who start off saying that generally end up being rude, but go on." She braced herself for what he had to say. She'd hate to have to tell him off but would if the need arose.

He blushed, scratching at one of his angry pimples. "It's just that… If I have to kill him, will I get paid more, like?"

Was *that* all he was worried about?

"Of *course* you fucking will. What do you take me for, a skinflint boss? I give bonuses, unlike Lenny, to people who go the extra mile. If you have to shoot that cunt in there, you'll get your due, don't you worry about that."

"Thanks. Sorry. For asking, I mean."

She had sympathy for him, and Dad's words came to mind. She'd repeat them to Jimmy so he knew she wasn't upset. "Don't *ever* be sorry for getting what's owed to you—don't work for free." She nudged him in the ribs to lighten things up. "Look, people who sit back and get taken for granted never get far—and you, Jimmy Lews, deserve to go far. You're a good bloke, you stuck by my dad, and asking for payment for services rendered isn't a bad thing. You do the work, you expect money, it's as simple as that. Anyone who doesn't want to pay you is a scumbag, and it's a reflection on them, not you."

He let out a rush of air, clearly relieved she hadn't bitten his head off. "How much?"

Cassie smiled. "See? You're learning. Twenty grand."

"Fuck me, that's what I would have asked for."

"There you go then. I'm a mind reader as well as a hard cow."

He nudged her in return. "You're all right, you are."

"I can be. On the other hand, you know full well how *not all right* I can be, so don't get too comfortable." Her phone bleeped, and she placed her cup down, moving away from Jimmy to read it. She checked the screen.

Shit. She *really* didn't need this.

Li Jun: *I am worried about my brother. Zhang Wei went out and has not come home. His wife, she is fretting. What do I tell her?*

Good old Li Jun. Despite probably knowing what had happened, he was still in her pocket. Cassie sighed. Hua, the wife, worked for Cassie, doing stints bagging the drugs sold at Li Jun's takeaway, the Jade Garden. Zhang Wei had distanced himself from the goings-on years ago by moving to the Moor estate and running The Golden Dragon. Hua was well aware of what went on in Cassie's world, and she'd keep her mouth shut if she knew Zhang Wei had 'disappeared', even if he *was* her husband, but in the meantime, she could cause a spot of bother if she wasn't aware of things as they stood now.

Cassie: *Tell her I'll visit her tomorrow sometime. Zhang caused problems. He's moved to China.*

Li Jun would know exactly what that meant. It was the same cover story for where Jiang, Zhang Wei's son, had gone. He'd been killed by some scrote, a machete slice to the neck, and it had been hushed up so people didn't ask questions about him no longer working at the Jade—where a load of drugs sat in an unplugged fridge, baggies sold with the fried rice.

Li Jun: *Oh no.*

Cassie: *Sorry, but you all know the deal. I'll get word out in* The Life *so people know where he is.*

Li Jun: *I am sorry it has come to this. I did not think my brother would escalate things.*

Cassie: *Well, he did, and that's the end of it.*

Li Jun: *How…?*

Cassie: *He was shot. It was quick. Now go and shut Hua up.*

She slipped her phone in her pocket and continued drinking her coffee, her arse against a cupboard. "Sometimes, I could really do with being a normal person." The admission surprised her, and it was weird: because it was Jimmy, she didn't want to take it back.

He gave her a sympathetic look. "Sorry you're not."

"Yeah, well, life has its own design for us. We're kidding ourselves if we think we can carve out our own destiny. Sway it, yes, but not completely direct it." That was a bit bleak, and too close to her showing him her soft side. She couldn't allow this conversation to continue so brought out her monster. "If you need to kill Jason, shoot him right in the eye. That's got to hurt." *Like it hurt Vance Johnson when Brenda gouged his out with a key.*

Jimmy winced. "Yeah."

"He deserves all the pain coming his way, the sneaky little wanker."

Buoyed by a fresh surge of adrenaline, she finished her drink and left Jimmy to it, driving to Mam's where she'd fill in the ledger and finally get some sleep, even if it was only a nap. Tomorrow lunchtime, she'd visit Hua, a woman who'd be mourning not only her son but her husband, her only close relative left Yenay, her daughter.

Tough. Zhang Wei should have known his place. It was his fault this had happened.

Pushy bastard.

Chapter Five

The text bleep going off on the work burner
pulled Brenda Nolan from sleep, propelling
her into an early morning she didn't want to see.
Who the chuff was WhatsApping her at this time?

Cassie: *Are you alone?*

Brenda: *Yes.*

Cassie: *I'm coming round. Now. Also alone.*

That was all Brenda needed to know. Shit had probably gone down regarding Karen Scholes. Either that or there was news of Jason. Brenda had told Cassie all about his little scheme—always best to be upfront with whoever paid your wages, wasn't it; thank God she'd gone down that route—and had been tense ever since, awaiting the outcome. Then there was her confession about Karen also wanting to take over the patch.

What a mess, but she'd rather this mess than one involving her to the point where *she* met a bad end. Survival, self-preservation, was uppermost in her mind, and she'd trample over whoever to ensure she remained safe. Loyalty to a friend meant jack shit when you risked being killed, and she had a lot of years left to live, thanks.

She swung out of bed a bit too enthusiastically, going giddy (damn her age). At the window, she opened the thermal-lined curtains and leant on the sill that was chilly from the winter freeze, the inside bottoms of the three panes covered in condensation, the outside smiles of snow. It still coated the ground, chunky flakes coming down. People had tromped through it on the paths yesterday, some kids fucking about with snowball fights, and the fresh fall had created mounds over and beside the footprints.

Tyre tracks imprinted the road, appearing dirty in places where the tarmac peeked through. Snow always changed this street, hiding the imperfections, the rubbish mounting up in the front gardens, giving the illusion it was like all the other, better roads on the estate. Come the thaw, the reality would be all too prevalent again: the council needed to do a clean-up; new windows, doors, the potholes fixed in the pavements, and people directed to the tip instead of using their gardens.

Why am I living here again?

Because you love the house.

She shivered and made to turn for the bathroom but caught sight of Sharon Barnett hammering on Karen's door, the orange light of a lamppost shining on her. Christ, she was up early. A barny at this time of the morning didn't bode well, *if* that was what the door-whacking was about; Sharon appeared angry enough. Or had Karen been dealt with and Sharon was panicking at not hearing from her?

Brenda shrugged, thinking she'd better get showered and dressed rather than go and see what the hassle was. Cassie would tell her soon enough.

Had something happened already, though? Cassie was obviously okay, not dead, she'd messaged Brenda—or had Karen killed her, stolen her phone, and pretended to be her? That would be weird but not surprising; Karen would want all of Cassie's contacts, wouldn't she.

"For fuck's sake."

Brenda slung her dressing gown on over her grey fleece pyjamas with polar bears on them, stuck the burner phone in a pocket, and ran downstairs—well, as much as someone her age could run when they smoked as many fags as she did. She shoved her feet into her fluffy boot slippers, lined with that teddy bear fur, and opened the door, switching on the outside light. Assaulted by the cold, she moved the dial on the heating to get it fired up and stepped onto her path. She'd cleared it yesterday, but it was blanketed now, the snow coming down like a maniac overnight.

"Fuck's sake *again*!" Annoyed, what with the pressure of Cassie coming round sitting on her shoulders, and no ciggie or caffeine yet, she took a deep breath. "Sharon?" It came out as a whisper-shout, phlegmy. She coughed to clear her throat. "Sharon!"

The woman in question spun from Karen's door and looked across. "She's not answering— the door or her phone. She *always* answers me."

Dread seeped into Brenda's belly, despite knowing Karen was going to get her comeuppance—it was still a shock when reality hit, even *with* forewarning. "Maybe she's having a lie-in."

The suggestion could be plausible. Cassie might not have offed Karen yet—and she planned to. She'd said so, something like: 'She'll be dealt with in the usual way.' That meant Marlene the Mincer.

Christ Almighty.

Sharon shook her head. "No. That's not like her, you know it isn't."

"Have you two had a falling out or something?" Brenda wrapped her dressing gown fronts around her and held them in place with a cuddle, tucking her fists beneath her armpits. God, she should have just minded her own bloody business. She could be drinking a brew and smoking by now, the radiators clonking while they heated. "Come over here, will you? We don't need the whole street listening."

Sharon—reluctant by the look of it—tromped from Karen's door and up Brenda's path, the snow creaking beneath her flimsy red slippers, the open-front kind. Was she mental coming out in those or what? Her toes were red from the cold, the ends an alarming purple that clashed with the neon-yellow nail polish. She'd shoehorned herself into dark skinny jeans and an orange chunky-knit jumper, and her hair sat in a bun on her crown.

Inside, gagging for a coffee and a fag to steady her nerves, Brenda led her to the kitchen, turning on the light. She scrolled the blind up above the sink then flicked the kettle on, anxious because Cassie would be here soon, and while the element crackled and rumbled, Sharon taking a seat at the table, Brenda sent her boss a message: *Sharon's here.*

Phone on the worktop farthest from her unwanted guest, Brenda got on with spooning instant coffee into two mugs—she couldn't wait for her machine to filter, it took at least twenty minutes. She ought to clean really, the plates and whatnot from last night's late dinner still sitting in the bowl ready for the dishwasher. She'd been too tired from looking after Sid Watson, one of her elderly marks, to bother loading it. "So, where's the fire? It's a bit early for this kind of malarky, isn't it?"

Sharon sighed, picking at a fingernail, the *tick, tick, tick* of it loud. "Look, I've got to talk to someone. There's stuff you don't know about Karen…"

I know plenty, duck. "Oh right." Feigning nonchalance came so easily. It had to when you worked for Cassie. A poker face was part of your armour, something she'd learnt while under Lenny's rule. *Never show your opponent what's on your mind until you're prepared to speak.* He'd said that to her once, and she'd taken it on board.

Sharon stuffed the fingernail between her teeth and ripped it off.

"Don't even *think* about spitting that on my floor, you dirty cow," Brenda said. "The bin's just there." She nodded to the grey flip-top by the internal door.

Sharon got up and disposed of the result of her gnawing, returning to her seat with a weary thump. "She's got some stupid scheme on the go, and I'm worried she's gone and done it."

"Done what?" *Will she admit it?*

"I know I said I needed to talk, but I can't say." Sharon studied the fruit bowl, maybe the already-going-brown bananas, a bunch that had *Ripens Over Time* on the bag.

Well, Brenda had only bought them two days ago, so that claim was a load of old bollocks. That was the thing with bananas. One minute they were green, and the next time you looked, they had bruises, the yellow stage a mystery.

She told herself off for letting her mind wander.

"I can't grass on her," Sharon reiterated.

Loyal to the last then. "Is that why you're panicking, walloping her door at ten to six in the chuffing morning?" Brenda added sugar. "I mean, it's enough to wake all the neighbours, and if Karen's 'scheme' is meant to be kept quiet, you haven't done a good job at making sure it stays that way."

"I didn't want fuck all to do with it, I said no when she asked me, I wasn't going to be in on it, but she'll do it anyroad. She's obsessed, that one."

"So because she hasn't answered your texts or her door, you think something's happened, is that it?" Brenda flinched at her phone going off.

She read the message from Cassie: *Perfect*.

What the fuck was going on?

"Yes." Sharon got up and opened the long pale-pink curtains in front of the back door, staring out at the garden, the fir tree branches in Mrs Roderick's border weighed down with snow, the bushes covered in a glaring white wig, an old lady's perm. "I should get hold of Cassie. Should never have kept this to myself. But Karen's my mate…"

Brenda sighed inwardly. Karen was supposedly *her* best mate, although Brenda had long since realised Karen only bothered with her when she wanted something. It didn't sting as much as it should, and Brenda had got used to only being needed when it was convenient. She acknowledged there and then that *she* hadn't been such a good friend herself. If she had, she'd have tried harder, gone to see Karen a bit more, but saying that, why should she when it was clear she wasn't wanted in that way anymore?

Life, it changed things. It got busy, and there wasn't enough time in the day to continue nurturing friendships. Neither of them were who they'd been when they'd first become pals.

"*Do* you get it, though?" Sharon's breath turned to condensation on the glass in the door, and she drew a sad face on it. "It's not like Karen is the same lately, is it. I mean, she barely comes to see you. Not being funny, but she *uses* you when I'm not available."

"Shit happens." Brenda poured water into the cups, thinking life didn't change *that* much.

Here they were, still talking like they were in their teens, going against their friend, although Brenda hadn't said owt bad. A trio of mates was never ideal. One always spoke about either of the others, then made out they didn't when faced with the person they'd slagged off. It wasn't Brenda's style these days, she was way past that, but how unsettling that Sharon had gone down that route now, a regression of sorts. Why bring that up? Why tell Brenda something that could potentially hurt her? Was she jealous Karen was mates with Brenda?

"And, wicked as it sounds, I was relieved when she turned to you," Sharon went on. "There's only so much of Karen you can take, know what I mean? She's got so arrogant as she's aged. Or more arrogant." Her cheeks flushed. "That sounded bad. But you must know what I'm saying. She can be a bit full-on, and recently, she's been even more so. I can't cope with her by myself—I don't *want* to cope with her. I'm getting on in years and just want a bit of peace and quiet, to leave my day job at the supermarket and edit *The Life*. I swear, if I could tell you what she's up to, I would, but if she pulls it off, I need to be on her good side."

Because you think she'll be running the patch.

Brenda added milk and stirred, using the time to think about what to say. She wouldn't go against Cassie, and that last text told her the boss had something she wanted to say to Sharon if she thought it was *perfect* the woman was here. "I don't need to know all the ins and outs—like you, I don't want to get involved with stuff if I can help it. I've got enough guilt trips of my own to deal with. Here, get this down you." She pushed a coffee across the worktop. "And let's not act like we're kids, talking about Karen in that way when she isn't here. I don't like it, never did; I only went along with it years ago because of some misguided idea that if I didn't, I wouldn't have friends. I've since realised I don't need them."

Brenda lit a fag and inhaled deeply. That was better.

The doorbell trilled, and her stomach rolled over. *Here we go.*

"That might be Karen." Sharon darted as if to rush from the room.

"It isn't. Stay put or sit back down." Brenda stuffed the work burner in her pocket so Sharon wasn't tempted to peek, left the room, closed the door, and hurried along the dark hallway, puffing on her ciggie. She flung the door open, automatically glancing up and down for nosy neighbours, and ushered Cassie inside.

Door shut, Cassie stamped snow from her boots onto the mat.

Brenda launched into the latest information, whispering, "Sharon's been trying to get hold of Karen—texting and banging on her door. She's guffing on about Karen being up to something and that she should have told you. We both know what that means."

Dark shadows sat beneath Cassie's eyes, evident by the light coming in from the lamp outside. "Makes sense she'd do that. It's why I'm here. About Karen. I can tell you both at the same time. Saves me having to repeat myself, doesn't it. In the kitchen, is she?"

Brenda nodded and followed Cassie into the room, taking another huge puff of her fag, her nerves strung to their limit. Sharon's eyes widened at the sight of the patch leader, and she staggered to the side, coffee in hand sloshing, and plonked down onto her chair.

"Morning. You look a bit peaky," Cassie said. "Like you've seen a ghost."

Brenda held back a chuckle at that. Sharon clearly hadn't expected Cassie to appear. Brenda would bet she'd entertained ideas of Cassie being killed overnight, so to see her now… Well, she *would* seem like a ghost.

"I-I-I… Oh, fucking hell." Sharon burst into tears.

Cassie stared at Brenda who shrugged and turned to the kettle again. Cassie sat opposite Sharon while Brenda made another coffee, and the tension in the air was so thick she swore she could touch it, hold it in her shaking hand. Silence ruled the time it took for her to finish the drink and take it to Cassie, then she collected her own and sat at the head of the table, leaning across to the worktop to pick up her cigarettes, and a lighter, the one with Paris written on the side and a picture of the Eiffel Tower, something she'd stolen from Sid last week. She had a habit of nicking things, even though she could afford them herself, and had been arrested for it once in her younger days.

"Right, I'll come straight out with it." Cassie glared at Sharon. "Karen's gone and got herself disappeared."

The shock on Sharon's face spread her features out with her watery eyes going massive and her mouth hanging open. The crows' feet bunched, a tear anchored in one, and her chin turned into a double. "W-what?"

"I'm warning you, *don't* play coy with me, Sharon. I didn't get to bed last night and I'm in no mood to play games." Cassie blew her coffee then sipped.

"I told her it wasn't right." Sharon wiped the tears from her cheeks, the nail with the missing tip standing out amongst the longer ones. Again with the neon-yellow polish. "I said I wanted nowt to do with it."

"But you didn't tell me." Cassie doodled on the tabletop with the pad of her thumb, and the action seemed portentous, the calm before a violent storm that would blow Brenda's kitchen up something chronic. "You didn't feel it was necessary to warn me that your best pal was going to *kill* me and my mam. Me, I can deal with that, but *Mam*? No fucking way. *No one* threatens her."

"She's off her rocker, obsessed with taking over," Sharon babbled. "Karen, I mean, not Francis. I'd *never* say owt mean about Francis."

Brenda doubted that, she'd been there when Sharon had badmouthed her in the past, but whatever. She gulped some coffee and burnt her tongue and the roof of her mouth. Christ, today was getting mankier by the second. The icing on the cake would be Sid dying when he hadn't withdrawn the money, something she got all of her victims to do, which she handed over for Cassie to launder, then received a percentage.

Sharon burbled on. "I told Karen it was stupid, that we're too old to be gallivanting around the estate now, issuing orders, but she was convinced she was owed the patch. Like, it was ours before Lenny came along and stole it. She's never been happy about that. Me? I was glad we didn't have to be bullies anymore. I never did like it. Editing *The Life* and listening out for trouble suits me, and that's all I want to do."

Cassie's stare gave Brenda the willies.

Shit, will she get rid of Sharon as well now? Will she expect me to help her like she did with Vance? Will Sharon end up in Marlene?

"I've decided not to do owt about you, Sharon," Cassie said, "so don't go shitting yourself all over Brenda's nice chair. I'm well aware you weren't prepared to go against me or Mam."

"How?" Sharon blinked, her eyelashes clogged with tears.

"Never you mind. So long as you keep this shit to yourself, you're golden. If you need to chat about it, do it with me, Mam, or Brenda here. No one else. Do I make myself clear?"

Sharon nodded. "I won't breathe a word."

"I can see you won't, considering you didn't warn me about what Karen was up to. A sneaky secret-keeper, that's what you are—so make sure you remain that way with everyone else. Although, if you hear of someone wanting to take over the patch, or owt whatsoever to do with me or Mam, or even Brenda, you'd better tell me."

Even me? Brenda was well chuffed to be included, to be that important to Cassie.

The patch leader slapped the table. "This is your first and only warning, got it?"

Sharon whined, covered her eyes, and sobbed.

Cassie glanced at Brenda and rolled her eyes. Brenda gave her a smile and stubbed her ciggie out, immediately lighting a second. She blew smoke away from her guests (she wasn't *that* much of a heathen), and took another draw of her drink, willing the caffeine and nicotine to keep her on an even keel.

First and only warning. Sharon had better behave, or she'd find herself in the same situation as Karen.

Sharon lifted her head and dragged her hands down her face, resting them either side of her untouched coffee. Drips were already drying on the outside of the mug where she'd spilt it, and there'd be a ring stain on the table, which irritated Brenda. She whipped a tea towel off the side and cleaned up the mess.

"What…what happened?" Sharon asked.

You were clumsy, that's what happened. I swear, if this stain doesn't come off…

Cassie focused on Sharon instead of Brenda's frantic wiping. "Do you really want to know?"

"Yes."

"Fair enough. I wrecked her face with my weapon—Karen was unrecognisable by the time I'd finished with her. Lots of blood. My associate slashed her cheeks with a knife. We'd planned to impale her on The Beast's tail, like Karen had in store for me—fitting to turn her idea back round onto her, I reckon—but in the end, she had her throat slit, her stomach stabbed, and Marlene dealt with her after that."

Sharon let out a weird noise, half screech, half groan. "My God…"

"She shouldn't have overstepped the mark. Let it be a lesson to you." Cassie drank her coffee as though she hadn't just described something hideous.

Brenda shivered and sucked on her fag. Fucking hell, it sounded like they'd gone to town on Karen, overboard even. Who was the associate? Francis? Jason? Was Cassie saving his comeuppance for when she had solid proof of what he had in mind?

"Go home, Sharon," Cassie said. "And from now on, you'll be dealing with Doreen Prince when it comes to *The Life*. She's taken over writing it. I don't need your input, as in, you won't be meeting up with her to discuss the articles. Just edit them when she emails them to you."

Sharon's mouth sagged. "What?"

"You heard me." Cassie scowled. "If you're worried about your five hundred a week, it's safe." A pause. "For now. You'll continue to be

115

my ears—and you'd better get listening, else I'll start suspecting *you're* not on the level an' all." She waved at the door absently. "Say nowt about Karen. You'll understand what you *can* say once you've received the next instalment of *The Life*. Go on, piss off, I need a private chat with Brenda."

That had the coffee in Brenda's stomach all but curdling. A private chat?

Sharon rose and stumbled out, a muffled "Oh!" escaping from behind the hand over her mouth. The shock of everything had properly set in, and she undoubtedly wondered how she was going to convince people she didn't know owt about Karen 'moving away', because Brenda knew that was code in *The Life* for 'dead'.

The front door snicked shut.

Cassie sighed. "What a stupid fucking cow."

Brenda couldn't argue with that. "She sounded genuine when she told me she didn't want owt to do with it, though."

"I agree—someone else told me the same thing. Sharon's on her last legs with me. One more misdemeanour, no matter how small, and I'll have her. I can't be doing with baggy lips— unless they're giving me information. Now then…" Cassie twisted to face Brenda. "I'll be adding another five hundred to your weekly wage. I want you to keep an eye on Sharon. Get friendlier with her—that'll be easy because she'll need someone to fill the void Karen's murder has created, plus she'll be at a loose end, what with not having any meetings about *The Life*. I want you to monitor what she's up to in case she decides to do a Karen on me."

"Fine by me. She said she's giving up the supermarket, so she'll be even more lost. I'll make a habit of nipping over there each day before I go and see Sid. Act like I'm concerned about her."

"Good. The private thing I need to discuss… You won't be seeing Jason around anymore."

Oh shit. She's gone and done it already. Is that why she's got bags under her eyes? Was she up all night killing him and Karen? "Has he disappeared?"

"Not yet, I've got him somewhere, but put it this way, he won't be leaving that place alive."

"He's a bampot." It was what Cassie would expect her to say.

"That he is. I need to you pay as much attention as you can to Gina, too. That mother of his has the potential to cause a ruckus during the time he's 'missing'. I've no doubt she'll come whinging to me, asking if I know where he is, but she'll get short shrift until *I'm* ready to tell her he's dead. I know full well she won't take to you suddenly wanting to be pals, so I don't expect that of you—she's a closed door when it comes to friendships, isn't she. Always has thought herself better than everyone else, yet she lives on the shittiest street of the Barrington. Weird, that."

"I heard she likes her house and doesn't want to leave it." Brenda knew that feeling well. The location might be ropey, but the interior was what became home. "Jason told me that once— why he thought I'd want to know is anyone's guess. He wanted to rent somewhere else once he started working for Lenny and got better wages, but Gina wouldn't hear of it."

"Well, that's her lookout. You can't expect people to believe you're royalty yet live in the slums, can you. Anyroad, she'll know exactly what her precious son has been up to—and if she gives me any bother, I'll let her know where her husband ended up an' all."

Bloody hell… "Lenny…"

Cassie nodded. "Between you and me, Dad got rid of him for Jason's sake, said he was better off without that sort of man in his life. Do you know what really boils my piss? The fact Dad watched out for Jason, tried to make up for him not having a father anymore. Showing him what a proper dad was like. And look what Jason did. Threw it back in his face by wanting to run the patch. All his talk of us two dating—he was stringing me along, I see that now. He wanted to be with me, and all so he could be close by to drug me and Mam so we'd be off our tits enough that he could take over, making it look like we were incompetent."

"How wrong he was." Brenda drank some coffee, thinking about her new tasks. Dealing with Sharon was a breeze, but earwigging with Gina? Not a chance. The woman had her nose so far in the air it touched God's arsehole.

"Yep, and now he's paying the price for it." Cassie smiled. "He's currently attached to the floor by an eight-inch nail through his shin."

"Fuck me." Nauseated, Brenda imagined the pain, the blood. She was well aware of how wicked Cassie could be, she'd witnessed it first-hand with Vance, but Jesus Christ, a nail? Eight inches? She rubbed her goosebumped arms.

"He deserves it." Cassie swigged her coffee then stood. "Right, I've got a full day ahead of me and no chance of it letting up, so I'll leave you be."

She walked out, leaving Brenda staring at the chair she'd occupied. Jason held in place like that filled her mind, and she had to shut it down, get rid of the visual. She couldn't afford to linger on what he was going through. Like she'd always said, she was loyal to whoever ran the patch, and at the moment it was Cassie. No way was Brenda going to allow herself to feel sorry for the little scrag. But a part of her did regardless, despite his brash behaviour, his ego, his know-it-all attitude. He'd been a kid once, innocent, and she couldn't help but wonder if Lenny's influence had turned him towards the Devil even more than Jason's father's treatment of him.

Blimey. Emotions were a weird bunch, weren't they.

Chapter Six

The Barrington Life - Your Weekly

KAREN SCHOLES STEPS DOWN

Doreen Prince - All Things Crime in our Time
Sharon Barnett - Chief Editor

EMERGENCY EDITION. FEBRUARY 2021

Karen Scholes has decided to step down as our reporter. I, Doreen Prince, will be taking over. Karen has moved on from the Barrington, going farther up north to live a quieter life now she's getting on a bit. Her children may soon follow their mother if they query Karen's decision.

You understand what I'm saying, don't you?

Thought so.

In other news, Zhang Wei has decided to move away, too, so he can be with his son, Jiang, in China. Once again, please don't bombard the family with questions. Hua and Yenay have no intention of going back, so be respectful of their feelings and mind your own business. There's no information about what will happen to The Golden Dragon on the Moor estate, but that's not our concern anyroad because we use the Jade Garden, don't we.

Have a nice day.

Chapter Seven

These days, DCI Robin Gorley (he'd never think of himself without that title, he'd worked so hard to get it), came to his allotment every day, in all weathers, the only exception if there was a family gathering, a wedding or the like, and then he nipped there at the end of the party, loving the late-evening silence after the noise and sheer exhaustion he experienced with so many people around him, so many voices, so much of that awful thumping and screeching they called music.

Give him classical any day. A bit of Wagner smoothed his ruffled feathers.

Peace. He just wanted a bit of peace. Was it too much to ask after a long career fighting crime? Didn't he deserve a calmer existence, where getting up at Oh-God o'clock didn't feature, his alarm blessedly silent, him only rolling out of bed when *he* wanted to?

He'd admit he missed it, the hustle and bustle, the rush he'd always got when on the search for a criminal. Everything seemed so…empty now. He was a pointless human being, with nowt better to do than sit in his shed and think.

It didn't matter that snow now painted the ground, or that it was cold enough to freeze a witch's tit, as his mother would have said. He dropped by the allotment for some serenity away from a wife who'd badgered him throughout his career about not being at home much, not being a 'present father or husband', and she still did it now, harping on and on. He'd told her once that she'd known what she'd signed up for when she'd married a copper, but clearly, she hadn't realised the truth of that at first.

Melinda's ranting pushed him to escape her, when all along, his retirement was supposed to be about them reconnecting, making up for the lost time he'd spent on case after case. He'd pledged that promise to her years ago to stop her from leaving him—"I swear, if you don't give us some attention, we're going, Robin, do you understand?"—but he'd inevitably broken it.

Or maybe she'd forced him to with her constant jibes.

This morning, never one to not make a point when she could, she'd said, "You spend just as much time away from me now as you did before you left your job. What are you doing at that bloody allotment, because it certainly isn't growing owt at the moment bar a few fucking runner beans? Got a fancy piece on the go, have you?"

Like he would. Melinda would have his guts for garters if she found out—and she would, her friends were gossips—and besides, his downstairs equipment wasn't working like it should nowadays, what with his age. He'd blame brewer's droop but didn't drink that much, years seeing the results of drunken fights outside the pubs in town putting him off, and the Viagra Melinda had suggested didn't sit well with him.

128

"So you're saying you don't want to do it with me anymore, is that it?" she'd screeched.

And his mind had screeched back: *Please, please, just be quiet.*

He hadn't verbalised his thought, instead walking out of their kitchen, his three flasks of coffee cradled to his fast-narrowing chest instead of its wide form when he'd been in his prime, coming here to sit in his little shed, his sanctuary with two pictures on a whiteboard like the one in the incident room, names written down and red arrows pointing to clues—well, supposition, suspicions he'd had back in the day but hadn't said them out loud regarding a couple of cases that still bothered him.

The small heater warmed his toes, the aroma of gas from the cannister tainting the air, and he held a coffee from one of his flasks. He always made enough to last him for hours, plus brought a packed lunch along, although he hadn't had time to make that today. Melinda had started on him as he'd twisted the cup on the third flask, and he'd legged it to get away from her complaints. Still, Gregg's had been open, and he'd treated himself to some sausage rolls and a couple of glazed ring doughnuts. That'd see him right.

What he hadn't told his wife was that certain cases still haunted him, ones he'd never been able to solve—or one in particular he hadn't been allowed to. She'd go mad if he admitted he thought about them: "God, just let it *go*, Robin!" Despite his desire for peace, he wished he was still at work, sitting at a desk going over old crimes, desperate to find whoever had remained elusive, especially now Lenny Grafton was dead. One case had always concerned him, the disappearance then murder of Jessica Wilson, a three-year-old belonging to Joe and Lou, the farmers out at Handel.

There had been rumours that Lenny had dealt with the killer. Rumours. Who was Robin kidding? He knew full well Lenny had murdered The Mechanic, and Robin had taken a backhander and risked his job to hand over Jess' wellies and raincoat out of the evidence store— *stealing* it, for fuck's sake, a copper turned rogue, and it had left more than a rancid taste in his mouth.

Robin had shit bricks, worrying every day since that he'd get caught for it, reminding himself there hadn't been CCTV in the store back then to point the finger at him, but he'd been frightened of Lenny more than any camera. The man had been a right mad bastard, and Robin hadn't wanted to die by his hand—or that Marlene woman's. He'd tried to work out who she was, find her, but that name had to be a fake one. Surprisingly, no residents in town were called Marlene.

The holiday in Tenerife, paid for in cash with the bribe money, hadn't been as enjoyable as Robin had hoped. He'd thought time away would erase what he'd done, bring him and Melinda closer, but he'd been grumpy and out of sorts, the constant reminder that the holiday was paid for with ill-gotten gains turning the array of cocktails sour on his tongue, the good food curdling in his belly, the laughter of his wife and children somehow exacerbating his guilt-drenched emotions.

With Lenny having his heart attack and dying recently, Robin had breathed a massive sigh of relief—awful, absolutely awful to be glad someone was dead, but there you have it. Robin was free now, but that didn't mean he'd stopped thinking about Jess, or how he'd fobbed her mother off that time—the unpleasantness of that gave him nightmares, the woman coming after him in his dreams, begging him to find a clue, no matter how small, so they could catch the bastards. As far as he was aware, no one else knew what he'd done, and the knowledge had died with the former patch leader. Still, Robin shouldn't have taken Lenny's word for it that The Mechanic was responsible, nor should he have urged his superior to shut the case down, as per Lenny's instructions, Robin's reasoning being there had never been any leads apart from the white van, the person in the back, and the man in a balaclava wielding a firearm, and those had turned into dead ends.

Rear Van Man, as Robin thought of him, was still at large. Lenny had never approached Robin with information to the contrary, and Robin had scoured each *The Life* for hidden messages, ones Lenny had told Karen Scholes to write, but nowt had stood out. Someone out there still had to pay for their part in what had happened to Jess, but it wasn't Robin's responsibility anymore, and when it had been, he'd shushed it up through fear of Lenny turning nasty on him.

Or on Melinda and the children.

There was no way he could have explained things to Lou, therefore, he'd waved her concerns away as if they didn't matter, crippling himself with remorse over it at the time and every day since.

There was something else his wife wasn't aware of. That he'd worked so hard, gone out to cover shit up for Lenny off shift, so she wasn't killed, so their kids didn't meet Marlene. How could he tell her, though? She thought he was a true copper, blue running through his veins, not one as bent as a nine-bob note.

Ever since Jess' case had been closed, Robin had avoided Lou Wilson as much as he could after that cringe-inducing meeting where she'd wanted answers. The woman was broken yet determined, and the times she'd looked at him in The Donny once Jess had been laid to rest, well, it had scored a slice in his heart, and he'd wanted to tell her: "See that man you're with, the one paying for all the drinks? Lenny fucking Grafton? *He* stopped me looking for Jess. The problem lies with him, not me."

There was no doubt about it—she was right; her silent stare of reproach before she'd left the interview room that final time was right. He'd failed her, failed that child, and Joe. Himself. And all because he feared Lenny Grafton, feared the man telling the superintendent about what Robin had done with that evidence, feared for his family's lives.

So, Melinda rambling on at him… It was nowt compared to the remorse prodding him more and more each day. That was the problem with retiring. You had more time to think, your mind less full of cases, and it always strayed to what he *should* have done—ploughing on to find Rear Van Man despite Lenny telling him to 'back the fuck off or you'll regret it'.

Jess' ghost haunted him. He swore he saw her every so often, always three years old, always in that bloody rainbow coat and those pink wellies. She appeared in the market, weaving between the stalls, a bag of sweets clutched tight—Jazzles. In The Donny, perched on a barstool, a packet of cheese and onion Walkers in her hand. In the Jade Garden, stretching her chubby mitts up to the counter to take a lollipop from Li Jun, always a pink one. And every time, no matter where she was, she glanced over her shoulder at Robin and frowned, her stare as reproachful as her mother's.

That frown cut him to the bone: *You didn't find me in time. You listened to Uncle Lenny.*

Robin placed his cup down and wiped the tears from his cheeks. "Dear God…"

He took a shuddering deep breath and stood from his deckchair, his back clicking along with his knees. Sixty-odd but feeling eighty. He folded the chair and leant it against the wall. Shuffled to look out of the little dusty window.

Barney Lipton, a seventy-something and sprightlier than Robin, his bald head covered by a red beanie (complete with a white bobble on top, one his wife had knitted for him), was over the way in his plastic-paned greenhouse, tending to the plants he managed to keep alive even in winter. He had a knack with growing, did

Barney, installing a heating system in there that mimicked good weather, the warmth of the sun. He passed runner beans to Robin every now and then, who gave them to Melinda, never putting her straight that he hadn't grown them.

Another lie to add to his long list.

A tap on the shed door startled him—it was rare for anyone to come here, apart from other gardeners, and Barney was the only one around at the minute. Robin remained where he was, ignoring the intrusion into his retrospective thoughts. Barney glanced over. His eyes widened, and he dipped his head and tugged at a length of bamboo cane as if he didn't want owt to do with the person who'd come calling.

Odd. Unless it was that prat from the council, the one who'd warned them the allotment might be closed down. Perkins, his name was. A jobsworth.

Another knock, and Robin sighed. For Pete's sake, not only did his mind and his wife insist on keeping him from peace, a visitor did as well. He went to draw the chain across—you couldn't be too careful, and he should know, being an ex-copper, so he'd put one on a while back—then changed his mind about undoing it. Better to keep it there and face whoever it was through the gap.

Speaking to them meant letting all the heat out, and he tsked at that.

He opened the door as much as it could go, two to three inches, and his heart sank, skipping a beat or five, his tummy flipping. Lou Wilson stood there, her eyes nowt like they usually were (sad and lifeless when she wasn't looking at him or venomous with hatred for him when she was). Today they held anger, and he reckoned it glinted, warning him this wasn't a nice and friendly social visit. When would that ever be true, though? She detested him, and he couldn't blame her.

Shit.

"Yes?" he said, annoyed his voice shook.

As far as she was aware, he was beyond reproach, so why had she come?

She straightened her sparrow shoulders. "Let me in. I want a word, and it's been a long time coming."

Fuck, had she found out it was him who'd suppressed the case? He was sure he'd worded it in their meeting so it was ambiguous as to who'd pushed to close it down. Had DC Simon Knight and DS Lisa Codderidge blabbed to her? Lisa, definitely, because she'd been well upset at the time. Now there was no fear of Robin reprimanding them, now he wasn't their superior, they might well have spoken to Lou.

Thick as thieves, those two, and having a long-standing affair to boot.

You couldn't trust anyone these days, could you.

They hadn't known why he'd had to get the case closed, just that he'd done it, but it stood out a mile it had been his idea. They hadn't been best pleased. A waste of all that hard work, they'd said, plus there was letting the kidnap accomplice get away with it, allowing him to do it again to some other kiddie.

"What's the problem, Lou?" He used his police voice, the one that had him sounding authoritative, in control, when really, inside he was losing it.

"You know damn well what the problem is."

Lou stepped away from the gap and, oh God, Francis Grafton appeared. Had Lenny told her about Robin's part in Jess' case and she'd kept quiet? Now he was dead, had she decided to spill the beans to her friend, relieved to relinquish the burden?

"Open up," Francis said, her eyes narrowed, no sign of grief about her. Anyone would think her husband was still alive the way she glared at Robin.

She'd always been all-business, though. Always stoic beside her husband. Seemed his death hadn't changed her.

Robin swallowed and took the chain away, pulling the door wider. Francis and Lou stepped inside, cramping the place up and, further adding to the claustrophobia, Cassie entered.

Robin groaned. He'd heard the rumours through Melinda about how this young woman had taken over the estate with her brand of warped reasoning. Lenny was one thing, a force to be reckoned with, but Cassie was apparently a tornado, whipping up a tsunami that soaked the town.

"You may well moan," Lou said. "Because the past has caught up with you, fucker."

Chapter Eight

Lou's weapon sat in her bag, which she'd strapped diagonally over her torso to save it swinging around with what she had in mind. She'd taken a leaf out of Cassie's book and created her own murder tool this morning while her nephew, Ben, mucked the pigs out instead of her husband.

Joe worked part-time at the meat factory again now, and while today wasn't one of his shifts, the recently appointed newer manager, Marcus James, had phoned in sick, something about his teenager bringing home the lurgy from sixth form. Joe had to go in, of course he did, and Ben had come to take over his chores, meaning he'd lost his day off.

It suited Lou down to the ground. Fate couldn't have helped her out more if it'd tried. She hoped Marcus was off for longer, say a week, then she could get the coppers done over with Joe right out of the way, none the wiser. She'd be home in time today to cook dinner—they'd driven here at ten a.m.—so plenty of hours left to mince Gorley. Or set fire to him like Cassie wanted. Whatever happened, so long as he was dead by the end of it, Lou didn't care. They'd come here via the outskirts, no cameras to catch their images or Cassie's stolen car with the fake plates, no people other than Barney Lipton tending to his plants.

Ben, God bless him, wasn't the cleverest of souls, so Lou swanning off during the day, well, he wouldn't take much notice, his mind full of those Xbox games he liked to play well into the night. All right, maybe he'd wonder why she'd suddenly taken to leaving the farm when she usually remained there by choice, only venturing out when Joe urged her, but she doubted he'd dwell on it.

"It's not good for you, hiding out here all the time. Let's go and have a bevvy at The Donny." Joe said that every now and then, concerned she remained inside too much.

And he was right. Although it was a chore to leave the farm, to get ready and plaster on a fake smile, she felt marginally better once she was away from it.

Her memories went with her, though.

She snapped out of her thoughts and crowded Gorley, Francis and Cassie at her back. Their presence bolstered the steel in her spine, giving her the extra courage to proceed.

It was bloody stifling with four bodies and a gas heater going full blast, and sweat sprang out in Lou's armpits.

"Stick the lamp on." She pointed at a swan-neck black one on the wooden bench going along the back of the shed, opposite the door.

Gorley frowned, blinking, not doing as she'd asked. "What?"

Lou ignored him. He was a frail bugger now, a withered version of his former upright self. She glanced to her left, startled by an image of Jess on a whiteboard above the bench. Or was that her mind playing tricks? What was this, his own little investigation room? Or did he have that picture for other, more sinister reasons?

Yes, he did.

She jerked a thumb in Jess' direction. "What the *hell* is my child doing on there? What *are* you, some kind of *paedo*?" God, he ran a ring, didn't he, had set up a website where freaks of nature logged on and stared at kiddies. She was sure of it. "Is that why you're always in this shed? Do you come here to fiddle with your fucking filthy self, you bastard?"

Gorley spluttered, shaking his head.

He was rejecting her truth. No wonder he lived in a nice house on New Barrington. He got subscription money off pervs to pay the big mortgage. They handed over their money to him, and he sent them indecent images. That had to be it, didn't it?

Another photograph of a child, a brown-haired boy, was pinned next to Jess with a small circular magnet—pink. The final insult, Gorley choosing her daughter's favourite colour. She studied the image. Wasn't that the lad who'd gone missing, Lee Scrubs, an almost-teenager who'd told his friends he was going to run away because his dad was a bully? Lee had turned up dead in a ditch on the land the New Barrington now stood on, years before Jess had died, and the whole town had been horrified.

She ignored the red arrows and writing.

"You dirty ponce." She wanted to attack Gorley with her bare hands like she had with Vance Johnson but held back. "Francis, stand by that window so old nosy bollocks out there doesn't see."

"He won't say owt even if does, he's on the payroll as ears, but maybe we'll save him the shock." Francis blocked the view, and the shed darkened. "We don't need another body on our hands, death by a sodding heart attack."

Gorley whimpered and fumbled with the lamp, no denial about being a kiddie pervert coming out of him—*he can't even give me that*—and the time he was taking to find the switch was doing Lou's head in, stretching her nerves then shrinking them so the shrivel gave her goosebumps. She clenched her fists and her teeth, counting to three, telling herself if she got to five, Gorley would know about it.

At last, the shed lit up, Jess and Lee drowned in light, their innocent, stuck-in-time faces gazing on. Gorley stared at Lou as if about to shit himself. His silly grey fringe, usually held back with Brylcreem, flopped forward to cover one eye.

Good. She wanted him to experience fear like Jess had.

Like herself and Joe had.

He pushed his hair back. "Please, I don't know what you think I've done…"

Was he the man in the back of the van? Is that why he was never found?

My God, he's been walking amongst us all this time, the absolute wanker.

Her mind accepted that as a complete fact—it was the only reasonable explanation in her eyes, akin to her pretending Jess was in Cornwall— *she's still down there on the beach with her bucket and spade*—a story she made up to cope.

It cemented itself in her mind. Yes, Robin had clutched Jess to him, his dirty pig hand over her mouth to stop her screaming. Robin was the one they were after. No matter that Jess had wandered from The Mechanic's house to Sculptor's Field, Vance intercepting, as Cassie had explained. Robin had let her out of that home office, he'd encouraged her to her death.

Yes, that was how it had happened.

"You let my daughter down." She unzipped her bag and eased her hand inside, careful not to jab herself on the weapon—she didn't need any of her blood left here. Forensics were so good these days, who knew if it'd still be found in the ashes? "Twenty-three years I've thought about this day, told myself I'd come and see you, get things off my chest, and here I am. I can't hold it in any longer. I need *justice*."

Gorley's mouth flapped. Any more of that, and his creamy dentures would pop out. "I'm sorry, but there were circumstances—"

"Yes, we know about the bribe," Cassie said on a sigh, reversing and planting her back to the door.

Cassie hadn't gone to bed. Instead, she'd read the RESIDENTS ledger, then looked the coppers' names up in the others to see what Lenny had written about them. This bastard here, he'd suppressed the case—on Lenny's orders—so no wonder the person in the back of the van had never been found (*but it's Robin, that's why*). Lenny hadn't found him either; maybe he'd known the DCI was the accomplice after all—and if he wasn't, what the hell was he *thinking*, getting the case shut down? If Lenny were alive today, she'd use her weapon on him, no matter that they'd been good friends. He'd had no right to interfere, to cover for a bent copper, a paedo. When Cassie had told her about the information found in the ledgers, all Lou's suspicions had been confirmed. How come Cassie and Francis hadn't remembered this before now? They'd both read all the ledgers.

Maybe there was so much data it had slipped their minds.

Thinking of Gorley's wicked part in this brought on a surge of anger, topping up the rage that was already present, boiling it so her face flushed with heat, prickled with sweat. "You told your superintendent the case was going nowhere. How the hell have you lived with yourself?"

Gorley rubbed his wrinkled forehead, his liver-spotted hand jolting from the shakes. "Sleepless nights, guilt, you name it, I've been through it. Lenny was a nasty piece of work. He threatened my wife, my kids. What would *you* do in that situation?"

"What was *right*." Although she *would* have done everything to protect Jess and Joe, she wasn't about to say so. In his position, yes, she'd have gone down the same path as him, but that wasn't the issue here. "Someone's still walking around out there, a man or woman who held my child in the back of a van, maybe too tightly because she wiggled, screamed for her mammy and daddy. It was *you*, wasn't it."

Gorley winced, leaning on the bench. "I can't apologise enough for— Oh, my chest..."

So he was admitting it then. He hadn't denied being in that van. "No, you *can't* say sorry enough."

She felt about in her bag, slipping her hand inside the brown leather loop she'd created on the back of a five-by-three-inch piece of wood—the brown to match the gloves of the accomplice— *Robin's gloves*—a reminder to her of what this was all about. She'd cut one of her old belts down, attaching it to the back. The weapon sat across her knuckles now, nice and snug, no room for slippage.

"No amount of apologising will make this better," she said. "I've had to live without my child instead of seeing her turn into a woman. Your treachery, your *selfishness* in ignoring what was right to save your own children meant you got to see them grow up." Her heart hurt, but not from stress or the pressure of this situation. It was from missing Jess. "Enjoy their first day at school, did you? All those birthday parties? All those times they came to you for advice or needed a cuddle?"

"I'm sor—"

"Don't." She used her free hand to slice the air. "Don't you *dare* say it again. If you were sorry, you'd have kept working on it behind the scenes, quietly, no matter what Lenny threatened." That was a low blow, but she was past caring about how she manipulated things to suit her now. This was about her little girl, and she'd fight to avenge her murder until her dying day. "No matter that you were the one in that van."

She pulled her hand out of the bag and held it up. Gorley's eyes bugged, and Cassie whispered, "Fuck me…" Francis laughed, the sound creeping over Lou's shoulder—yes, Francis would approve, Lou had known that when she'd fashioned the bloody thing. At the thought of her friend's response, she'd chuckled to herself with every whack of the hammer, the extra-hard smacks she'd had to give so the leather was secure.

Twenty-three long nails stuck out of the wood, one for each year of torment without Jess, all of them matte, the grey colour representing her soul, how it had dulled the moment she'd known her baby wasn't coming home. The darkness of them reminded her of her thoughts, the ones where she'd planned for a day like this, the scheming keeping her from going even madder than she already was. And the brown leather loop, that was to show what goes around comes around, full circle.

No one else would understand. But it didn't matter so long as *she* did.

"What…what are you going to…?" Gorley pressed himself in a corner created by the bench and the wall, trying to get away. A stack of black plastic plant pots fell off, hitting the floor, black peat spilling out of the top one.

Peat… Lou shuddered, a distant memory poking her.

Gorley panted. "Someone will know I'm dead eventually, if that's what you plan on doing. Think about it. A policeman."

"*Ex*-policeman. And *no one* will know," Cassie said. "Don't tell me you're not aware of how we work, or is that something else you've conveniently tossed out of that sick mind of yours? Did Lenny ever tell you who Marlene is? Were you in with him that much that he let you know about her?"

Gorley shook his head, his cheeks a tad pasty. "All I did was steal the wellies and the coat, then get the case closed. I steered clear of Lenny unless he called on me to cover things up."

"Or to scare kids." Cassie stepped forward and stood shoulder to shoulder with Lou. "Like when they nicked drugs from Lenny's runner that time, and you came to warn them off. Why did he do that? Why use you? I've always wondered, haven't you, Mam?"

Francis nodded.

Cassie continued. "He usually sorted shit himself. What did he need *you* for?"

Gorley panted again and rested a hand over his heart. "Oh God. My chest hurts."

"Not as much as I do," Lou sniped. "Carry on."

Gorley's fingers turned onto bird's feet, curved, all disjointed and branch-like. "Lenny…he did it to keep me in his pocket. To remind me he was always *there*, that I had to obey him like everyone else did. He fucked with minds—and enjoyed it, you lot should know that. Look, can we chat about this? Do I need to be hit with that…that *thing* to make you feel better, Lou? Really?"

She suspected he was using a copper tactic on her: keep the criminal talking while he thought of what to do next. Any minute, he'd try humanising himself, like she was a *psychopath* or something, one who needed to be drawn out of her crazy head, him calming her down, the hero. Honestly, like she was even a nutter.

She glared at him. "Yes, it'll make me feel better."

Lou raised her arm, drew it back, the nail tips pointing in his direction, and thought of all the years helping Joe to muck out the pigs, the constant shovelling up of mess, her biceps strong, her back muscles well able to handle what she was about to do. She might be older now, she might be as skinny as Barney Lipton's rake, but she *could* hurt this man. She *could* kill him.

The adrenaline rush from another time, how she'd feared being caught, how Doreen had stared at her, blood dripping down her young face from the splashback, winged through Lou. The feeling of euphoria and power had thundered through her back then. It was doing it now, pushing her on, as was Jess' little giggle inside her head.

Go on, Mammy, kill the naughty man. Be The Piggy Farmer.

Lou launched her fist at him, and he raised his arm to block the attack, something she hadn't anticipated. It was too packed in the shed for him to get away, but he screamed and shoved her back regardless, using the arm she'd struck, driving the nails deeper. His dark shirtsleeve hid any blood and the sight of the gore she so longed to see, and she stumbled in reverse, Cassie steadying her with a fierce grip on her shoulders.

Lou wrenched the nails out, and with Gorley bent over, clutching the twenty-three wounds, scream-growling, lips tight together, she swung the weapon in a sideways arc, ramming it into his cheek, the momentum wrenching his head to the left. This time, his scream didn't come from an open mouth but one clamped shut by nails in his gums. His eyes bulged, his skin going purple, the cords in his neck rising, straining. Blood poured, trailing over his jawline and onto the side of his throat in rivulets, his head back against the side of the shed beside a newspaper clipping with the headline: CHILD GOES MISSING. One elbow propped on the bench stopped him from falling onto his skinny arse, and she was surprised he hadn't passed out.

He cried, tears mingling with the blood, and stared at her with true fear in his eyes, a cornered animal—and he *was* an animal. She smiled at another of Jess' ghostly giggles and, hand on his forehead, bracing herself for what she was about to do, ripped the nails out then sliced down. His wail filled the space, his cheek tearing into macabre, claw-like downward slashes, and he choked, spat a tooth out along with a stream of saliva-laced blood. Francis laughed with Jess, and Lou stepped back, readying herself for another attack.

She walloped him again, the nails driving into his throat, slight resistance at the Adam's apple, and she pushed with all her body weight, Cassie pressing in from behind, until the base of the nails hit skin. The breath from the gurgle spluttering out of him spattered Lou's face with warm blood that gushed between his lips, and he brought a hand up to clasp her wrist.

Please… She thought he'd whispered that, asking her with his eyes to keep the nails where they were. Taking them out would create so much damage. And death.

Cassie karate-chopped his arm, and he let Lou go. Lou snatched the nails out, blood arcing, water through a colander, falling to his shirt, on her coat, one errant stream casting a few dotted lines on the wooden side of the shed. Cassie moved out of the way, and Lou took a step or two back, watching him slump to the floor—*fascinating*—his hands scrabbling to stop the blood, his scarlet-soaked, ruined face skewed in pain.

Cassie took Lou's prime spot and loomed over him. "It's been said you never cross a Grafton, but as you've gathered, you don't cross a Wilson either." She turned to Francis. "Go and speak to Barney, make sure he remembers the score. Tell him to fuck off until tomorrow. Give him that envelope I put in the car door cubby."

Francis squeezed outside, closing the door, and Lou moved to the window, her back to it, and studied a steadily dying Gorley. Blood seeped between his fingers at his throat, and down from his wrecked cheek to drip onto the back of his wrist. He whimpered, groaned, air sawing out of him, painful rasps, ones Jess might have released while Vance had strangled her.

It was enough to urge Lou to kick out at Gorley, the thick sole of her sturdy farm boot connecting with his nose. The sickening—*beautiful*—crunch of bone and cartilage gave her immense satisfaction, a sound she'd play over and over in her head on the nights she became an insomniac. She kicked again and again, like those kids you saw on the telly, an episode of *Crimewatch*, caught on CCTV beating someone up. With each strike, the back of his head whacked the wall, his hand dropping from his neck to rest on his thigh. Blood still pulsed, faster now, from fear, she hoped, and her last assault saw her boot breaking through the threads of skin holding his cheek together, the toe tip lodged in his mouth between his molars.

She lowered her foot to the floor. Looked at Jess on the whiteboard.

I'm doing it all for you, my little darling. All for you.

Jess laughed.

Chapter Nine

The Barrington Life – Your Weekly

FOR PETE'S SAKE, STOP SENDING BLOODY
FLOWERS!

Karen Scholes – All Things Crime in our Time

Sharon Barnett – Chief Editor

JULY 1997

Look, you know what was said in a previous version of *The Life*. Joe and Lou don't want any flowers — stop getting them delivered to the farm. Spend the money on your own kids, or grandchildren, like they wanted. How come you're so intent on sending bouquets, paying out for them, when it took me getting seriously arsey to make you all donate towards the horse-and-carriage hearse? (Which, I might add, was a damn sight more important than a few roses and carnations.)

How do you think Lou feels, seeing reminders that her little girl has gone, all those bunches in vases? You mean well, I get that, but pack it in. Lenny will be having a word with everyone who sends any after this, so consider yourselves warned. Betty from Blooms will be keeping a record of all purchases.

Likewise, no visitors to the farm — you know who you are. Lou can't handle it. Anyone who turns up will get their lights punched out.

Behave.

Two weeks after the funeral, Lou stared at a kitchen full of half-dying flowers, their smell cloying, the varying scents getting down her throat. People had sent them, maybe hoping they'd make her feel better. She couldn't stand them, all those petals, the colours, the leaves. Joe had bought her a bunch a week right from the beginning of their relationship, but she'd have to tell him not to bother now. She hadn't told him, back when he'd presented her with bouquets, why she didn't want to receive them, why each one stirred unrest inside her. It was a part of her past she'd never reveal to him; flowers were something she'd prefer not to receive.

They were a painful reminder of what had happened, back then and now.

She'd compost them. Later.

Lou had remained in the house since the funeral, but a few people had dropped by. She hadn't opened the door but stared out of the window at them clutching Pyrex dishes full of food. She'd been unable to summon the energy to listen to their condolences all over again and had phoned Lenny to ask him to put a stop to the visits and the flowers. It was all too much.

Today she had a meeting, one she'd asked for in private, with those three detectives, the ones who led the case, useless prats that they were. DCI Robin Gorley, DC Simon Knight, and DS Lisa Codderidge. Bob Holworth was going to be there, too, seeing as he was a beat officer, supposedly with his twig-like finger on the pulse of the community, although he turned a blind eye to everything because of Lenny. Joe wasn't aware of what she was doing—she didn't need him smoothing things over, accepting everything the police had to say, nodding, saying, "Thank you for all you've done."

And what was that then? Nowt much as far as she was concerned. Officers had gone over Joe's land and Sculptor's Field, canvassed the residents, but other than that…

It wasn't enough.

Part of her thought Joe was amenable for a quiet life, or maybe coping with grief was enough for him to deal with at the minute, and owt more was too…extra. He was probably holding on by the skin of his teeth, although he hid it well for her sake, God bless him. She could understand why he acted that way, but for her own peace of mind, she needed to know once and for all whether everything had been done that could be done—but she knew that answer already: it hadn't, not in her mind anyroad.

The lie in place—"I'm going to the market, Joe. I need some fresh air and time by myself. No, please don't come with me…"—she parked in town behind the high street and walked towards the nearby police station. She imagined they'd be dreading her arrival, moaning amongst themselves about having to put up with some snivelling woman who couldn't let things go. The Family Liaison Officer, Dina Corsa, had been the only one who'd seemed to give a proper shit, staying with Lou and Joe while their horrific new life played out, from the snatch right up until a week after the funeral—but her being there was more to do with watching them, to see if owt slipped and their guilt became apparent.

It was usually the parents, Dina had said, without tact, but Lou preferred honesty.

"Not that I think it's you, mind." Dina had massaged her temples—it must be headache-inducing having to observe people so closely. "But I have to stay here because of that line of enquiry. You're good people, I can see that, but those are the rules, and I apologise if it's obvious I'm listening in. I'm not meant to tell you this sort of thing, by the way."

Well, it was a good job Lou hadn't taken offence at that, wasn't it. She'd seen enough programmes on the box that showed a behind-the-scenes look at how the police worked. She remembered thinking they wouldn't find a speck of evidence against her and Joe: "You carry on and do your job, Dina, but you won't see or hear owt incriminating from us."

She sighed, blotting out the memories.

Along the path that had a shortcut branching off it into town, people gave her funny looks—some who might think Lou and Joe had something to do with the kidnap and murder, others clearly at a loss, not knowing what to do or say:

"Do I smile at her? No, that'd be disrespectful."

"Do I ask how she is? No, because I don't want her going on and on then crying; I can't deal with that, got too many of my own problems to deal with."

Really, though? The biggest problem you could ever have was dying yourself or someone you loved carked it, but she got it, she did. She'd avoided grieving people herself in the past, unable to express her condolences without feeling fake or inappropriate. Like the flowers, platitudes were a waste of time. Nowt made death any better.

Unless it was murder for justice.

But maybe knowing the man in the back of the van had been caught…that would go some way to easing things a bit, to calming her tumultuous mind. Lenny had already killed The Mechanic, the man who'd wielded the gun, but she'd keep her mouth shut about that.

She entered the station, approaching the desk, telling the sergeant behind it who she was and why she was there, a stream of words she'd rather not have uttered, but they were necessary all the same. To be honest, talking was a chore now.

Being a human trying to move on while emotionally stuck in place wore her out.

He gave her a sympathetic glance, his top lip hidden beneath a wiry, ginger-tipped moustache, the roots brown, and buzzed her through, his directions on where to go leaving her mind as quickly as they'd entered it. She only ever retained information that was important these days, and all of it was to do with Jess.

The sergeant must have phoned through. DCI Gorley appeared in a doorway on the right, hanging out of the room, balanced on one foot as if he gripped the inside jamb, swinging there, a child in a man's forty-something body. Hardly appropriate or respectful behaviour, was it, but she'd let it slide no matter how much it poked at her nerves.

In the room, the other male officers sat on a sofa, the woman on one of two armchairs. Lou had been in here before, the 'soft' interview room, one that was supposed to put people at ease and fool them into thinking they weren't being interrogated. Comfort, Gorley had said last time: "So you don't feel overwhelmed with a table-and-chair setting, and we have video recording us instead of the usual tape."

She wondered whether they'd be recording this today, whether they'd indulge her with the idea of catching her out. Whether her name was below the word SUSPECT? on their incident room whiteboard, never mind that Dina would have passed on her expert opinion, proclaiming them innocent.

"Please, take a seat." Gorley pointed to the spare chair.

Clearly, he wasn't in the mood to be polite and shake her hand today, and the other officers weren't inclined to use their manners either, remaining on their arses instead of standing when she'd walked in.

Lou couldn't help but feel the seat left for her was so she could be seen from all angles, her responses scrutinised, her body language interpreted to fill whatever mould they wanted it to fit in. Well, they could study her all they liked, she hadn't killed her daughter, so they could piss off on that one.

She sat, regardless of her stubborn nature urging her to insist she'd stand, thanks, and placed her handbag on her lap. They'd probably see that as her putting a barrier between herself and them, some kind of psychological nonsense, but no, she just didn't want it on the floor. Who knew how many germs it'd pick up there. She had to ensure her home was free of dirt for when Jess returned from Cornwall.

"How can we help you today?" Gorley sat beside Bob on the sofa. He crossed his legs and laced his fingers, cuddling his knee with them, his shiny-shoed foot swinging.

"The man in the back of the van." Lou stared at him. "Or woman. They still haven't been found. Why not?"

Gorley winced at her directness and cleared his throat, his cheeks going rosy. "Ah, see, here's the thing…"

DS Lisa Codderidge leant forward in the chair opposite, hands curled over the ends of the arms. "Please know we didn't want this to happen." She gestured to herself then DC Simon Knight.

Gorley glared at her, his nostrils flaring.

It reminded Lou of the pigs on the farm.

"I'll handle this, thank you." Gorley appeared uncomfortable, either annoyed at Codderidge or bracing himself for what he had to say. Was bad news on the way? "Jess' case has been closed for the time being."

Blood pulsed in Lou's ears, and the room seemed to spin. Disorientated for a moment, she blinked. "What?" She hadn't said it breathily, on a gasp, a mother at the beginning of a long road who just wanted to curl up and die, but more in anger, a blunt delivery through clenched teeth.

"We will still be looking out for Rear Van Man, and of course the one who had the gun, but as of today, the

*team has been disbanded. The clues we have to go on —
the people involved, the white van, the shotgun —
that's all we have, nowt else. There were no traces on
Jess or her clothing to lead us to whoever took her. I'm
sorry."*

*"So she's only just been put in the ground and
already you're giving up?" Lou couldn't believe this.
Didn't her daughter matter? Now she was buried, the
case was being buried, too?*

*"As I said, we will still be active — well, I will be;
Simon, Lisa, Dina, and Bob will need to return to
normal duty — but I assure you, if I find owt, you'll be
the first to know." Gorley swallowed.*

*"What's your reasoning behind this?" she asked.
"I've heard about cases being active for years. Why is
Jess' so different?"*

*Gorley smiled as though he'd armed himself with
this information previous to the meeting and was well
able to fob her off. "With so little clues to go on, the*

search of your husband's land and Sculptor's Field bringing up absolutely nowt regarding a perpetrator, despite the body being left by The Beast… We have no van sightings other than Joe following it as far as he could, then it disappeared on the Barrington, as you know. No discarded shotgun, boilersuit, balaclava, or the brown gloves from Rear Van Man, no witnesses coming forward saying they saw someone on the field placing Jess there. We're chasing ghosts."

"You're washing your hands of it, you mean." Lou had a hard time remaining in her chair. She gripped the top of her bag, the contents hard against her fingertips—the back of her brush, perhaps, the can of Coke she'd brought in case her throat went dry.

Codderidge wasn't successful in hiding a smirk; was she glad Lou had sniped at her boss? But was it really the best time to chalk up slights? Was it appropriate? No, it bloody well wasn't. Lou was offended by it. Wanted to leap up and hurt the woman:

Don't you dare sully the meeting about my daughter with your stupid, stupid one-upmanship, you fucking bitch!

Codderidge maybe sensed Lou's animosity and straightened her treacherous face into something more respectful. "Despite not being on the case any longer, myself, and Simon especially, will be keeping our eyes and ears open. There must be something out there for us to find."

My thoughts exactly, although I still don't trust you, woman. Why haven't you found it already? You've had long enough. Too busy shagging your colleague, I'll bet.

"Um, that's not what the superintendent wants," Gorley butted in, hand held up to stop Codderidge from talking. "We've unfortunately had our orders."

So had someone else made the call? Was Gorley only passing information on and the decision was nowt to do with him? She'd heard of 'don't shoot the messenger', of course she had, but right this second, if she had a gun, she'd fire all six bullets into his bastard face.

Lou rose, unable to stand these people any longer, their presence, their breathing, their everything. Yet she stared at each officer in turn, wanting to gauge where they stood on this, the tiny root of revenge grasping in the darkest corner of her mind, a course of action she'd take if she had to, but for now, she'd just think about it, imagine it.

A life for a life. Or four lives for Jess'.

Maybe five if the superintendent found himself on her shit list.

Gorley couldn't meet her intense gaze, glancing around the room like some builder totting up the cost of repairs, already mentally absent from the discussion now she'd made her intention to leave clear. He'd washed his hands of her as well as her daughter.

Knight made eye contact and mouthed 'sorry', his cheeks reddening, then he perused the ceiling, mimicking Gorley enough that Lou was tempted to check for damp patches up there.

Codderidge gave her a tentative smile, her eyes apologising instead of her mouth, but those eyes, they didn't show her soul enough, the shutters to who she really was were closed, and Lou wasn't convinced the woman's emotions were sincere.

And Bob? He gawped at the cheap grey carpet, maybe asking himself why he hadn't gone inside the houses of the people he'd questioned after the kidnap — if he had, he could have been the hero of the hour and found who they were looking for. And as the strained seconds ticked by on the office-generic wall clock, the air tense with Lou's suppressed feelings, he was unaware she knew all about his part in this from the gossips at the funeral. She ought to blab about it, right this minute, tell Gorley what his precious officer hadn't done, but no, she'd wait, get her revenge someday.

She walked out, going down the corridor, back to the door to be buzzed through. She strutted into reception and leant on the front desk. "I'd like to see Superintendent Black, please. Now. Either that or I file a complaint."

The flustered desk sergeant made a phone call then escorted her back down the corridor, past the door to Soft Interview One, which stood open, the room empty, only the three shapes of backsides on the sofa giving any clue as to who had so recently sat on it. Up some stairs, and she was shown into an office, Black sitting behind a large desk covered in paperwork, his hair the opposite of his name, all grey-white with tufty sideburns, a leftover from the seventies. She supposed he was proud of his uniform by the way he straightened the tie. He was probably all togged up ready to do a press conference about closing the case.

He stood and shook her hand, his thin fingers unsettlingly warm, bordering on sweaty. "Ah, you had a meeting with DCI Gorley et cetera, yes? Do sit down."

Lou didn't want to. She wiped her palm on her thigh. "I'll stand and get straight to the point. I'm not pleased the case has been shut down."

"Well, it hasn't been closed exactly, just scaled right back. DCI Gorley is still on it."

She laughed, the sound abrupt and unlike her usual, the one before Jess was taken, where every note was carefree and merry then. "What can one man do that a hundred or so couldn't? If your whole force couldn't find any clues, how will he?"

"I do understand your feelings, I really do, but unfortunately, when no new clues come to light, and the ones we currently have lead nowhere, we can't possibly keep a whole force on just one case. There are budgets and—"

"So it comes down to money. The cost."

"I'm afraid that's a factor, yes. When I asked DCI Gorley how things were progressing and he laid it all out, the decision was made to scale it back."

"But she hasn't even been dead that long. It's all so fresh."

"To you, I imagine it will always be fresh, and I'm incredibly sorry about that, but to us... We've exhausted all options. I can ask DCI Gorley to question the residents again, if you like, but it will be a long process as he'll have to do that around his usual workload. Other crime doesn't stop because one little girl is dead."

Oh.

Oh.

That was a terrible thing to say. So unfeeling. So blunt.

She mentally wrote his name on her shit list.

Bright-red pen.

Capital letters.

At the top, above Gorley.

"So he'll fit it in," she said. "Like an afterthought. I see how it is."

Lou stalked out, anger burning through her. These coppers, they didn't care. And despite Codderidge acting like she gave a shit, she didn't, not really. Her behaviour had been to keep Lou from casting the net of blame over her, to absolve her of any involvement in the decision to shut the case down.

All of them would pay. Black, Gorley, Knight, Codderidge, and that bastard Holworth. She just didn't know how.

Yet.

Chapter Ten

Cassie's gloves had her hands sweating; maybe a pinch of fear contributed to that, too, although it was healthy fear, the kind that whispered: *Don't be complacent. Don't think you'll never get caught.*

The allotment was on the outskirts of the estate behind the trees near where one set of her sex workers stood at night, and someone could come by, cutting through town on their way to Worksop, spot the shed burning, the smoke rising, and call the fire brigade. While that wasn't what she wanted or needed, she'd leave it up to fate.

Gorley was dead, main objective met.

She took his notebook off the bench, lit the edge via the gas heater, and dropped it on the shed floor, searching for something to place on top. She spotted a folded deckchair leaning against the wall and chucked it onto the mini fire. The flames caught the striped material, an orange tongue poking through, the smell plasticky. Once a good blaze was going, enough that it wasn't likely to go out, she glanced at the ex-copper and thought about his adult kids mentioned in the ledger. His wife.

Then shut her mind off.

She walked out, closed the door, padlocked it, and joined Mam and Lou in the car.

They needed to get away before the gas cannister exploded.

She took a blonde curly wig off the passenger seat, left there once they'd arrived at the shed, jammed it on, and checked Mam and Lou in the back. They also had wigs on, disguised perfectly again for the journey. If they *had* been seen on the way here, their fake descriptions were so far removed from their usual that the police would be looking for illusions. She drove off, the air tense, adrenaline barking at her blood, and scanned the road behind and ahead for anyone who'd spot them.

No other vehicles on the quiet lane. She was going to enter the town from the far side of New Barrington, where the scrappy bloke conducted his sometimes-illegal business. She'd have to get this stolen vehicle torched then wrecked. Blood had splashed on her and Lou, and it was on Lou's boot where she'd kicked Gorley's cheek.

Barney Lipton had been sent away, a grand in his pocket instead of a flea in his ear, his silence guaranteed; he'd been one of Dad's many listeners back in the day, a spy in The Donny. The RESIDENTS ledger said Barney had been used to watch Gorley on the allotment once the old DCI had retired. Lenny still hadn't trusted the ex-copper then, even though it appeared the man had done as her dad wanted.

Cassie had made the decision not to mince Gorley, not to keep the detectives' deaths quiet. During the early hours (possibly an hour of madness, depending on how this turned out), she'd decided the coppers getting killed was a proper good message, that even officers of the law weren't safe—not that she'd be admitting she'd had owt to do with it, but people might suspect.

If they got to Simon Knight and Lisa Codderidge this evening at their usual liaison spot, where they had sex then went home to their spouses, the officers looking into Gorley's shed fire would rush to the other crime scene. They'd be occupied, caught up in officers killed in the line of affair, not duty, while Cassie, Mam, and Lou scoffed cake from The Shoppe Pudding, something Cassie needed to pick up later.

At the breaker's yard, she parked where the scrappy waved her to, a spot with space around it, and everyone got out, keeping their wigs on. He came over, smiling, blow torch in hand, and opened the passenger door. A quick blast, and the seat caught fire.

"Crush it afterwards," Cassie told him and walked off, Mam and Lou in tow.

Earlier, she'd hidden her car behind a large metal storage container, no questions asked, as always. They'd gone inside and put their disguises on, then she'd driven them to the allotment. Now, they all needed to put carrier bags over their shoes, especially Lou's boot, then they got in her car.

Cassie drove away, going over everything they'd done so far, her mental checklist, ending on CCTV. It wasn't a worry, and neither was the route she'd taken to the allotment. No one had been around, not even dog walkers or other drivers. Lenny was watching out for them above, paving the criminal way.

"I like your weapon." Cassie glanced at Lou in the rearview.

"It has meaning." Lou smiled her creepy smile and stared out of the window. She looked spookier than usual with that wig on, a short purple thing Mam had dug out of a locked chest in her wardrobe, one of many hair pieces nestled inside with sunglasses, sets of contact lenses, and leather gloves.

Had she used them when she'd worked the estate with Dad, pre-Cassie? Funny how Cassie had gone down the same route, buying her blonde wig to hide who she was for when she dropped Doreen Prince's money off on the weekly, although the subterfuge there could stop now as Doreen working for her was out in the open since she now wrote *The Life*.

I'm more like my mother than I realised.

Cassie headed for the farm, snatching her wig off and tossing it on the passenger seat. She hadn't left them in the stolen car to be burnt because totally trusting the scrappy wasn't something she was prepared to do. "Like I said briefly earlier, I want the police to know they've been targeted."

"Why the change of heart?" Mam asked beside Lou.

Cassie shrugged. "Because if they're busy with Gorley, Knight, and Codderidge, they won't be interested in the squat. Get your wigs off. We don't want anyone seeing us and associating them with my car."

"Oh, I didn't get a chance to tell you. That won't be a problem, the police." Mam took off her black curly wig, then nudged Lou to do the same with hers. "I received a phone call after I'd sent Barney on his way. The police car being close to the squat isn't an issue. The officer in question will make out he knocked on the door, getting no answer. On the back of my suggestion, and considering the cleaners covered the area with snow where the car was torched, our inside man is going down the route that Bob switched off the tracker at that location somehow, disposed of the vehicle, and started a new life elsewhere."

Cassie was well aware Mam wasn't mentioning the police contact's name. Didn't she fully trust Lou?

"But with Gorley being torched, and the other two being killed tonight, the pigs may well realise the cases are connected." Lou sniffed. "Not that I care about your decision to leave that load of scum where they died, but I do think it would have been better if Marlene was involved."

Has she lost some of her bravado? Is she realising we might get caught and she could go down for a stretch? It's a bit fucking late now.

"There are pluses to each scenario. Yes, my first instinct was to cover it all up..." Cassie wasn't about to admit to Lou she'd got rattled when she'd first seen Bob in the boot, hence him going to Marlene. "But then I thought of how we'd be sending a strong message. Twenty-three years have passed, yet still the job gets done—people will cotton on to the significance in the end, that all those four officers were on certain cases together, and maybe the police will come to question you because you were involved in one of them, so be prepared for that." Cassie wouldn't worry about it now. Like Dad had said, business first, worry later. She could be making the biggest mistake of her new role, but time would tell.

"He didn't need much persuading to do what I asked. The copper, I mean," Mam said, thankfully changing the subject. "Amazing what ten grand can do."

Cassie turned onto the farm track and drove around the back. She reversed by the mudroom door. Ben came out of the pig barn a few metres away and gazed over.

"Will he be an issue?" Mam asked.

"No," Lou said. "I told him I was going with you two for a coffee. God love him and everything, but he's a bit dim, easily persuaded to believe whatever I tell him. My brother's the same, his dad. Not the sharpest scissors at the salon."

"Okay." Cassie sighed, tired. She still had to go and see Hua, buy the cakes, and wanted a nap this afternoon. There was a chance she'd get to the squat. She'd warned Jimmy not to go outside for a fag until she'd given him the all-clear, and he'd let Shirl know to steer clear, too. Anyroad, Shirl was ill with the flu and wouldn't be a problem. "We'll meet up again later, as planned. What are you telling Joe?"

"That we're having a few drinks at your mam's place and I might stay over."

"That'll raise red flags, the staying over bit," Mam warned. "You never do that."

Lou shrugged. "Okay then, I'll come back home." She sounded mardy. A brat.

"But you'll have blood on you." Cassie frowned. Lou couldn't be thinking straight. "We'll put boilersuits on." Clearly, there was still a lot they needed to fine-tune. It was all very well knowing *how* they'd kill Knight and Codderidge, but the small print needed some tweaks. They'd been so intent on getting Gorley, they hadn't had time for an in-depth conflab about the other two.

That could lead to mistakes. She'd already made one by killing Nathan Abbot and didn't plan on doing that again.

"Fine. See you later." Lou got out.

She waved to Ben, who tromped back inside the barn scratching his head, maybe because Lou had carrier bags over her shoes, *shit*, and she entered the farmhouse, her shoulders straight, the usual slouch completely gone.

Bob's and Gorley's deaths had boosted her.

Mam switched to the passenger seat, and Cassie set off, glad to be away from the mental woman. The way Lou had behaved in the shed reminded Cassie of herself, her monster, and it was unsettling, akin to looking in a mirror and seeing all the parts of herself she didn't like. Parts she had to be in order to run the estate.

"She's not right in the head," Mam said. "Bats in the sodding belfry."

"You think? Fucking hell, she's always been weird, but…"

"I know. Look, let's get through this for her then forget about it. I've always felt guilty that I still had you and she didn't have Jess. The Mechanic planned to take you next, so thank God your dad stopped him before he could snatch you. So I owe it to Lou, this…this insane nonsense. I'm not much liking it, I have to say. Killing coppers is a bit too close to the bone for me, but hopefully, once she's killed them all, she'll calm down, stop overthinking everything."

"What she's doing will never bring Jess back, so why is she bothering? It's like she's righting a wrong that won't have the outcome she thinks it will—making everything better. Okay, I can see she's already stronger, and the murders will give her the sense of justice she's after, but will this be the end of it? Who else will she think of to blame? We could be killing people for months to come."

"No, I won't allow it, and neither should you." Mam smoothed her brunette hair which had gone cotton-woolly from the wig. "It's Knight and Codderidge, then she's got to accept we won't be entertaining owt else. You do realise that if she goes off by herself, like she did with Bob, you'll have to give her a warning, no matter who she is, and if she ignores *that*, she's dead."

Cassie hadn't even entertained that. Lou had been in her life from the start, was like an aunt, family—otherwise, Cassie would never have helped the woman to this extent. "But she's your friend. So much for 'Graftons don't squeal' with regards to people they love."

"They do on occasion, just that your dad preferred to be blinkered when it came to his mates. Lou doesn't get to break the rules. The only people who can get away with things is me and you—we'll cover up for each other. But anyone else? No, Lou is a resident, albeit not on the actual Barrington, but she's under your rule—Handel Farm is within your jurisdiction, so to speak. Besides, her and Joe wanted it that way."

Bloody hell. Mam was serious.

"Right. Then let's hope she doesn't fuck up after tonight." Cassie pulled into Mam's driveway.

In the hallway, they removed the carrier bags and their shoes, placing them inside a black rubbish bag along with their gloves. Cassie left it by the front door. They showered and changed, then went downstairs, and she added their clothing to the bag. She was trusting Lou to get rid of her own.

"I've got to speak to Hua so will be back in about an hour," Cassie said. "Have the police gone from the burn site?" She swiped up the black bag, needing to know the answer because she had to burn it and the contents at the squat.

"Yes. I didn't want to say an awful lot in front of Lou. Our new contact is DI Gary Branding, and he turned up there alone, saw no patrol car, and reported the location as vacant, that there must have been a glitch in the tracker for it to report Bob as being there. He didn't even get out and poke around and wrote in his report that no snow had been disturbed."

"Fine. So he replaces Gorley, yes?"

Mam nodded. "He's been hankering to help for years, so it was an easy decision to choose him."

"Then I'll pop in and visit Jason, burn this," she held up the bag, "and see if I can get some information out of him today. A confession."

"Good luck there." Mam smiled. "Make sure you get home quick. You need sleep to be on your game tonight."

Cassie nodded and left the house. She put the wigs in the bag and stuck it in the boot. In the car, she sighed with exhaustion, lethargy taking hold of her, but she pushed on, driving to the Jade despite her eyes hurting, gritty from lack of sleep. It was 'weigh day', and Hua would be in the office using the little scales and bagging the drugs—unless she was so upset about Zhang Wei she'd asked Yenay to do it.

She parked and used her key for the takeaway, seeing as it wasn't open yet. Noon was an hour and fifteen minutes away. Li Jun stood in the kitchen, and he peered through the rectangular cutout in the wall behind the counter, pausing in his task of slicing onions. His sons, the skinny Dequan and the chubby Tai, carved various meats on white plastic chopping boards. Yenay stirred the boiling rice in a huge steel pan on the hob, appearing lost in thought. That or the milky-looking water was mesmerising.

Cassie lifted the counter hatch and went into the kitchen. "Is Hua in the office?"

"Yes." Li Jun bobbed his head. "She is upset, as we all are."

"I can imagine."

Cassie glanced at his sons, who kept their heads down, expressions blank, then she eyed Yenay. The young woman didn't stare belligerently, as Cassie had thought she would. Instead, she appeared ashamed.

"I'm sorry," she said. "My dad shouldn't have done what he did. We all know the rules, and he broke one."

"I'm sorry, too." Cassie gave a taut smile. "But you know what has to happen when people don't toe the line. It was quick, he wouldn't have suffered, so there is that."

"Thank you." Yenay used a tea towel to lift the pot by the handles and moved to the sink.

Discussion over then.

Cassie walked into the office and closed the door. Hua sat at the desk, a pile of weed in a baking tray, small baggies, and the weighing scales on top. She peered across at Cassie, her eyes red, her cheeks swollen from crying. Up on her feet, she came to Cassie and hugged her, taking her aback.

"I am so humiliated by my husband's actions," she said. "Your father gave us a good life, and Zhang disrespected that. I love him, I will always love him, but I am disappointed in him."

Cassie pushed her away—gently, but she needed to separate them all the same. "He was doing what he thought was right. For his son. I understand that, but despite me telling him Jiang's death had been avenged, he wouldn't listen. He felt the killer's family had to pay. That's not how it works. If the rest of the family are innocent and know nothing of what their relation did, they remain alive; you get the same courtesy."

Hua slumped onto the chair, defeated, no doubt, confused as to why Zhang Wei had left their takeaway intent on badgering Cassie, trying to get her to see things his way. "He was crazed with grief. Did not know what he was doing."

"I imagine he was." *But he knew exactly what he was bloody doing.* "Have you seen *The Life*?"

Hua nodded, her fringe swaying, and she worried her hands. "Zhang has gone to China. I will always say this. When people ask, this is what I tell them."

Cassie believed her, but she had to ask, "Will there be any more problems? From you or Yenay? Li Jun? His wife and sons?"

Cassie didn't think Li Jun would dare, and his missus, Nuwa, had been the one to persuade him to work for Dad all those years ago, agreeing to the terms no matter what. They knew the rules, the whole lot of them, but they must be conflicted. They'd thought of Lenny as family, treated Cassie and Mam as such, too, yet a member of their *true* family had hurt the 'adopted' ones. It had to burn, having their loyalty tested like this.

Hua shook her head. "No. We will continue as we did when Jiang was murdered. As Li Jun says, we smile on the outside and cry on the inside." She gestured to the drugs. "I am here, as usual. I will always be here, the same day every week."

"And The Golden Dragon?"

"It is in my name, Zhang Wei wanted it that way. I will run it."

Satisfied this saga was over, Cassie left the room, nodding to Li Jun to let him know she'd drawn a line under the whole sorry business and no further action was needed. And that he mustn't bring this up again. Sad as it was, and much as she wanted to hug the old man, she couldn't linger here, nor could she allow herself to show sympathy in front of the family. Anyroad, she had cakes to buy and Jason to visit, then she could get some much-needed sleep.

She strode out and down the street to The Pudding. The bell jangled with her push on the door, and the usual scents of baking wafted around her, as always, reminding her of childhood when Lenny had brought her here.

What she wouldn't give to go back in time and relive those days.

Nicola Faraday, her dyed-black hair stuffed inside a net today, spray-painted the edges of some white icing roses with soft-pink dye. She glanced over the counter, a big smile in place to greet her customer, but stiffened upon seeing Cassie, that smile dropping. "Oh God…"

"Don't get your knickers in a twist, it's nowt to get in a bother about. I only want a coffee cake." She'd opted for Mam's favourite, knowing Lou also liked it. They'd sit at the island later and eat it, drinking champagne in celebration, and Cassie would remind Lou that this was it, over, no more deaths for Jess unless the man in the back of the van was found.

But Lou thinks it was Gorley. Barmy cow.

"Oh, okay." Nicola took a flat box from under the counter and set it up, her hands shaking.

Cassie had thought this before on her last visit, but Nicola was overly nervy around her, like she was hiding something. Of course, she could just be shitting bricks because Cassie presented herself as a hard bitch who'd barb your face if you looked at her wrong.

"Everything sorted from before?" Nicola asked.

Rude of her to ask, but Cassie wouldn't pick her up on it today. She was too tired. "Yes."

"Good. I didn't like the idea of there being trouble down here. Those kids haven't come back, the ones by the lamppost."

No, they wouldn't have, because Jason had bloody sent them here to keep the street clear so Brett Davis could rob drugs from the Jade, and Cassie had warned them to stay away. The fact that the robbery hadn't happened, and Jiang had been sliced with a machete instead, wasn't owt Nicola needed to know. She was the same as everyone else on the estate, under the impression Jiang was in China.

This woman here was fishing, that much was clear. Had Helen Davis, the woman who ran the nearby laundrette, Brett's aunt, been gossiping to Nicola while drunk? She'd better not have. Cassie had been sure the woman would keep her mouth shut about the Jiang murder business, seeing as her nephew was the one who'd killed him, but alcohol loosened lips, didn't it, and Helen wasn't known for keeping secrets.

Maybe Cassie needed to pay her another visit at some point to further establish the rules.

"No trouble," Cassie said. "Nowt for you to worry about anyroad. And the lads won't be hanging around out there anymore."

Nicola placed a coffee cake from the glass counter inside the box. "Doing owt nice tonight?" She indicated the cake.

"Me and Mam are having a night in with Lou. A few drinks, the cake."

"Oh. Nice."

Cassie didn't want to indulge in chitchat any longer so remained quiet while the sale was rung up and she paid. She said goodbye and left, sensing Nicola's stare on her back, but she didn't fret about it. Nicola was an older woman, had worked in her little shop for years under Lenny's reign, before that even. She'd be stupid to push it.

Cassie placed the cake box on the passenger seat then drove to the squat, parking around the back so if any pigs came along, despite DI Branding saying the area was clear, her car wouldn't be seen. She'd promised to message Jimmy and let him know if she was on her way, but she'd forgotten.

She WhatsApped him: *I'm here*.

Jimmy: *Okay.*

Watching all around her as she crept to the front of the house, and clutching the black bag, she let herself into the squat, the air tainted with something Jimmy must have cooked. Maybe instant noodles but definitely toast. She found him in the living room with Jason, who was awake, his face doing its best to heal, the blood and exposed flesh dried now. It appeared hard and uncomfortable, likely to crack if he tried to smile. His lip was worse, swollen and puffy. She'd sewn the slice in it tightly on purpose to give him maximum discomfort, extra pain to go along with that in his leg and face.

"Vuck ovv," he said, clearly having trouble speaking.

She laughed, couldn't stop it from roaring out, and Jimmy turned away to face the blind-covered window, grimacing. She dropped the bag and walked over to Jason, stared down at his ruined face, fascinated by the state of it, by the fact that *she'd* done this to him. The missing eyebrow and eyelids gave him a sinister air, some freak in an old-fashioned circus. Going by his body language, he hadn't even bothered to tense in anger at her arrival, just remained slumped. Maybe his leg was so agonising he didn't dare move.

"Are you ready to admit what you were going to do to me and Mam yet?"

He would have closed his eyes if he could, she was sure of it, shutting her out. How much was it getting to him being beneath her, so far down the pecking order now? His pride would be wounded more than his body. Him wanting to take over the estate was bad enough, but the lengths he was prepared to go to bothered her more. He'd planned to get them hooked on strong anti-depressants, drugging them so much they'd be in no fit state to work, then he'd take over as a 'kindness', all the while putting it about that they were so upset by Lenny's death it had rendered them incapable.

What a disgusting man. He'd faked who he really was to Lenny, making out he was a good sort, taking the advice and fatherly gestures, all the while plotting behind his counterfeit smile.

He mumbled something.

"What was that?" She crouched and reached out, poking his ravaged cheek, stony against her skin. "I didn't catch it."

He roared in pain, his free leg jerking north, his pinned one jolting at the thigh. His scream reached a higher decibel.

"I expect you're well sore," she shouted.

Jimmy coughed, his mind undoubtedly conjuring what she could be doing to Jason, but there was no more torture in their future, at least not at the minute. Jason's wail stopped abruptly, and he passed out, his head falling to one side. Fresh blood oozed on his shin. Idly, she wondered if his leg would go septic, if he'd eventually die from an infection if she didn't kill him first. She strode to the bag and snatched it up, going to the kitchen. Bag pushed inside the furnace, she took a knife out of the drawer, returning to slice Jason's trouser leg so she could get a good look at the wound.

Oh. The skin, as well as being a violent purple and swollen, was hairless. Did he *shave* them? What a strange bloke. And yes, something was definitely going on there with the start of an infection, yellow pus sitting around the nail head.

What did she care? He'd be dead soon anyroad.

Stupid dickhead, not keeping up with his tetanus jab.

She chuckled to herself and went to the living room doorway. "He's out of it again, Jim."

Her new employee turned to look at her. "What did you just do? I heard ripping."

She pointed at her captive.

Jimmy spun to give him his attention. "Oh shit, that's going nasty."

She supposed seeing the large round end of a big nail embedded into a shin bone *would* be nasty, but to her it was justice, Jason getting what was owed to him. She thought of Lou's weapon, all the nails. Funny how they'd both opted for those.

"It'll probably get worse as the hours go on." She shrugged. "I've got stuff to do until later tonight, but I'll nip back when it's dark. Maybe he'll be more inclined to speak to me by then."

"What do you want him to admit?"

"About drugging me and Mam, taking over, that's all he has to say to me. Simple really. I heard it on the recording but want him to say it to my face. Try and get him to drink some water if he wakes up. I don't want him dehydrated and dying on me. Right, I'm off. Catch you later."

Outside, she checked the road and general area, then dragged herself around the back. The driver's seat was heaven on her aching body, and she fired up the engine.

Home.

Sleep.

Then a double murder.

Chapter Eleven

Sharon Barnett was devastated, so much so her heart actually hurt with each beat, the area around it seeming hollow yet full of emotion at the same time, a confusing contrast. Karen, dead? It was surreal, felt untrue, yet there was no doubt she was gone.

Why had she been so *stupid*? Why couldn't she let the estate go and accept it was no longer hers? Christ, they'd had enough years of Lenny running the place to get used to it. Some online article said you only needed to see or do things seven times for them to become 'normal' to you, so why hadn't it worked for Karen? She'd always grumped about it, annoyed she hadn't thought of what he had, ways to keep everyone in line, plus generating such massive revenue.

Sharon had told her time and again that Lenny had a business head on him, and money he'd earnt from owning the meat factory and selling the drugs had enabled him to buy up houses one by one, create a vast fortune, purchase the high-rise, get a mortgage for Joe's wasted land, selling it off at a profit, purchasing Sculptor's Field. No way would Karen have been able to do all that. Her desire to swipe up Lenny's hard work, even going so far as to get Francis to sign all properties and money over to her—*such* a mad, ridiculous scheme—had meant her fatal downfall.

And now look, she'd been disappeared, supposedly moving farther north. Everyone knew damn well what that meant, and Sharon had been worried about having people coming round to ask questions now it had been aired in *The Life* (she'd cried so much while editing it for Doreen that she hadn't been able to see properly). But no one had turned up. Cassie must have got to them all, warning them to leave her alone. That or they weren't bothered Karen had left town. Some might even be glad.

Sharon stared out of her living room window at Karen's place. Well, she couldn't see it as such. A plain-sided, dusty white removal lorry had arrived outside it an hour or so ago, Cassie's people emptying the place, which basically told everyone just *how* Karen had disappeared, although the information in *The Life* had made it clear already. The residents knew what 'moving away' meant.

What about her kids? They'd be shocked but weren't silly enough to push Cassie for answers. Adults now, they were, and each rented a high-rise flat off Francis. A funny pair, they'd never seemed like they were Karen's, born to the wrong parents, aloof and distancing themselves as soon as they were old enough. They barely came round to see her, not liking her working for the Graftons; they were snooty and wanted to break away from her, as if their common-as-muck mother embarrassed them.

No, they wouldn't kick up a fuss. They'd be too bothered about how it would make them look to be associated with someone who'd needed to be dealt with in that way, ashamed their mam had done something so bad she'd had to be silenced.

Sharon would miss her pal despite being sick of her lately. They'd grown in different ways over the years, Karen stuck in time, thinking she was still young and able to boss her way around the Barrington as if she were in her twenties, well able to give someone a good old punch. Sharon, on the other hand, had mentally moved on from those days as soon as Lenny had appeared on the scene, glad she didn't have to bully people or poke her nose into their business. She'd made out she was still interested—she didn't want to get in Karen's bad books—but deep inside, she was tired of the drama. She'd preferred the times they'd taken a Victoria sponge round to houses and helped people through the bad days. Tea and cake, the fixer of all issues, not fists and mean words.

She'd been bloody lucky that Cassie had been lenient on her. Who'd told her Sharon was against taking the estate back and didn't want any part of it? Who even knew, apart from her and Karen, what her friend had planned to do? As far as Sharon was aware, it was between them, no one else involved. Someone had Sharon's back, and she'd like to thank them, but it wasn't likely she'd ever find out who it was.

Had Karen been whispering in certain people's ears without Sharon's knowledge, asking them if they'd switch allegiance should she retake the crown? Dangerous, that, and she couldn't imagine Karen being so lax in that department. People were loyal to Cassie and would run to her at the slightest sniff of foul play.

It had to be Brenda then, being a tall blade of grass—but then a grass she wasn't if she'd done it for Sharon's benefit, to stop Cassie hurting her.

Sharon wasn't dim, she knew damn well Karen had told Brenda shit she shouldn't have, sharing secrets that were supposed to be kept quiet because Lenny had ordered it. Sharon couldn't blame Brenda for opening her gob to Cassie. She'd been in deep with Lenny, classed as a friend as well as an employee, and she was in deep with Cassie an' all. Who'd go against either of them if it meant meeting that Marlene woman? That was one of the main reasons why Sharon hadn't wanted to reclaim the estate. She wanted to live, not be murdered by some unknown bint who must enjoy killing if she'd agreed to be paid to do it.

She shuddered and jumped at the sound of a man in a balaclava slamming the removal lorry's back doors shut. It could be classed as normal, the blokes in those woolly masks, considering it was snowing and so cold, but this was a message from

Cassie, showing the residents of the street just who was taking Karen's stuff away: *Look what happens when you break the rules*.

Sighing, Sharon left the window and switched the telly on, her Spam, gherkin, and brown sauce sandwich not settling too well in her stomach. Maybe the bread was the culprit. Wheat was a bit of a bugger to her as she'd aged, but then again, the vinegar from the gherkins probably wasn't helping, all that acid.

She hadn't bothered going into work, not after she'd received such bad news from Cassie, and anyroad, she'd be putting in her notice tomorrow. At last, she could retire, and besides, work wouldn't be the same without Karen there. They'd been in the supermarket from when it was a Kwik Save, but it was now an ASDA. So many memories. Best she end that chapter of her life and begin a new one.

She sat on the sofa and picked up her cheeky daytime vodka and tonic in lieu of a coffee (one of many she'd swigged), needing the alcohol to give her the strength to get through the coming minutes, hours, and days, getting used to a life without Karen in it.

Loneliness beckoned.

The local lunchtime news came on, *Look North*, with a blast of music that jarred Sharon's bones, and she sat bolt upright at a picture of Mr Plod, Bob Holworth, in the top-right corner, her heart rate thundering. A new, blonde newsreader faced the camera, her features rigid, displaying no emotion, perhaps readying herself to deliver the latest.

"A police officer has disappeared in suspicious circumstances. A source close to the investigation said his patrol car's last location was on the

B6079, heading towards Worksop. After that, they lost contact with him."

The woman stared at the viewers, stern, and a bit scary if Sharon were honest. She much preferred the weather lady. At least she cracked a smile.

"PC Bob Holworth's last visit was at Grafton's Meat Factory, one of his usual night shift patrol checks. Officers have been there to question the manager, Joe Wilson, who said: 'Nowt has happened here for a night-time police visit to be necessary. All alarms were still set this morning when I arrived, so no break-in.'" Stern Blonde blinked as Bob's image was exchanged for a pile of ash and wood, some bamboo canes in the background, sticking up as if waiting for a tent to cover them. "Also, earlier today, an allotment shed was burnt to the ground. A body was inside, that of ex-DCI Robin Gorley. With two police officers in the news, there's speculation the cases are linked."

She waffled some more, but Sharon wasn't listening. What was going on? She knew Bob well, had warned him of any scuffles that were about to go down on the estate so he could make himself scarce, keeping him from having to cover owt up. If he wasn't around when shit went down, he couldn't report owt to his superiors, could he. Not that he would, Lenny had got to him. And as for Gorley, she had no clue why he'd be dead, in a shed of all places.

While normal people would take this news about Bob as a copper disappearing in the usual sense, not Cassie's kind, people on the Barrington would know otherwise. Sharon was surprised it had made the news if Cassie had owt to do with it; she usually had things hushed up. Was she something to do with torching Gorley?

Which copper had blabbed to the press? Who had the bottle? And why would Bob need to vanish, Gorley set fire to? Had they gone against Cassie and she'd found out? Had Bob spotted something at the meat factory and threatened to tell all?

Sharon gulped her drink down and, despite her earlier remonstrations about no longer wanting to get involved in the weird, cult-like Barrington lot, old habits died hard, and she got up, stuffed her arms into her coat, and marched to Brenda's in her slippers. She knocked, her toes getting cold from the snow seeping between them, and wished she'd put her boots on. It had taken ages for her feet to thaw when she'd gone into Brenda's this morning.

Brenda opened up, her hair done in a nice chignon wotsit, a tight black leather catsuit covering a slender body Sharon had always been envious of. Without even saying a word, Brenda moved aside. Weird. If she didn't know what Sharon wanted, she usually *always* asked outright on the doorstep. Had she heard about Bob and Gorley, too?

Sharon entered and beelined straight for the kitchen. She sat in the chair she'd been in earlier and shuddered, Cassie's ghost sitting opposite, staring at her. Sharon blinked the woman's mirage away.

Brenda waltzed in and leant against the worktop, arms beneath her tits. "What's the matter?" She'd said it kindly. Maybe she thought Sharon needed a shoulder, a cup of tea and a slice of cake now Karen was gone.

No Victoria sponge or PG Tips would fix this.

"Bob's disappeared, and that Gorley copper's been found burnt to death in his bloody shed."

Brenda frowned, her mind cogs working. "Bob? Which one? I know a few of those."

"Mr *Plod*."

Eyes wide, Brenda swallowed and glanced at the wall clock. "Oh shit. How did *you* find out?"

"It was on the news. Bob was driving towards Worksop then vanished."

"I thought you meant *proper* disappeared." Brenda huffed out a laugh. "Maybe he's decided to fuck off—his missus is a right rum one, he's probably had enough. What do you care?"

"I was just curious, and maybe Cassie needs to be told."

"Trying to remain in her good books, are you?"

Sharon's face flamed. "Well, yes, but she did tell me I had to keep my ears open, didn't she. If *she* disappeared Bob and Gorley, why the fuck is it on the telly? A police source gave information. Someone's leaking shit out."

She told Brenda the rest, hoping she asked her to stay for the afternoon so she didn't have to go home and face the rest of the day without Karen, but with Brenda all dolled up, that wasn't likely.

Spooked by what Sharon had told her, and worried life on the Barrington was about to get hairy if people were dropping Cassie in the shit—if she'd had owt to do with Bob and Gorley—Brenda left the kitchen and went into the living room, shutting the door. She swiped her work burner up off the coffee table and phoned Cassie—fuck sending one of the coded messages. This could be classed as a life-or-death situation, couldn't it? Or extremely dangerous anyroad.

It rang several times, then, "What's the matter?" Cassie asked.

"Bob Holworth. DCI Gorley, that wanker bloke. It was on the news Bob's disappeared and Gorley's been torched."

"What?" Cassie didn't screech, just uttered that word in a dull tone. She was angry, that much was certain.

"Do you think someone's doing it to make a claim on the patch? Like, they're causing trouble to let you know they're around, showing you what they can do? It can't be Jason, given what you told me, unless he's in on it with someone else and they're doing stuff on his behalf."

"Fucking hell, the last thing I need is another person challenging me. How did you find out about the pigs?"

"Sharon's come round and told me; she's still here and wanted me to pass it on to you." Brenda was dying to ask if Cassie was involved but didn't dare. "What shall I tell her?"

"That it's nowt to do with me."

Oh. So who's going round after coppers then? "It mentioned Bob had been at your factory, and Joe told them there wasn't a break-in or owt. Just so you know, like. Sorry to say this, but why didn't Joe tell you? The police might go to your mam's, sniffing, asking questions."

"Fuck's sake. Thanks for this. I'll warn Mam."

The line went dead, and Brenda had a strong feeling Cassie knew exactly where Bob was, despite saying she'd had no hand in it. The question was, why had Bob and Gorley been dealt with? Bob had been the patch policeman for bloody years, always looking the other way if things went pear-shaped, always fudging his reports so owt nefarious wasn't documented. Never had he seemed to want to piss Lenny or Cassie off. And Gorley, though a lecherous wanker (he'd tried it on with Brenda once in The

241

Donny, and she'd stamped on his foot with her high heel, reminding him he had a wife called Melinda), had steered clear of owt Barrington-related if he could help it, except with Jess, of course, and he couldn't very well bow out of that. She'd long suspected he was in Lenny's pay.

Two policemen, gone. Earlier, Cassie had said she hadn't had any sleep. Had she just lied to Brenda, making out she was innocent in all this? Had she dealt with Karen and Jason, then moved on to the two sides of bacon?

If so, why?

"Don't get involved, you daft cow," she muttered and slid her burner into her bra; a tight fit, but she couldn't leave it lying around now Sharon was here.

Once, Brenda had caught her rooting through her knicker drawer, claiming she was after toilet roll when she'd gone upstairs for a wee. An unlikely story, because who the fuck kept loo roll in with their undies? Sharon had been snooping, simple as that, and Brenda suspected Karen had told Sharon about fleecing the old men and she was looking for money. Karen said no way, but Brenda's suspicions wouldn't go quiet.

In the kitchen, she took two mugs off the wooden tree and poured coffee from her carafe. Added whitener and sugar. Handed Sharon one. "Cassie hasn't got any idea what's happened, so if anyone asks, that's your answer."

"Is that the true answer, though?" Sharon sipped. "Cheers for this, by the way. I've had a few vodkas since I last saw you."

"Shock, I assume."

Sharon nodded.

Brenda sighed. "If Cassie says it's nowt to do with her, who are we to question it? I mean, come on, are you going to confront her, demand answers?"

Sharon shook her head. "Not bloody likely. If she's going after coppers, she'll have good reason. I'm keeping my nose out of it and my mouth shut."

"Hmm, best you do."

Brenda ought to do the same but was desperate to know what was going on. Maybe Cassie would confide in her at some point. They'd got closer lately. Lenny used to tell Brenda things, so maybe his daughter would follow in his footsteps. Until then, Brenda would keep *her* nose out and her head down.

The thought of having an eight-inch nail put through her leg kind of helped her make that decision.

Chapter Twelve

"**I** need to come in."

Doreen stared at Cassie on her doorstep. The woman's wavy red hair was gone, in its place a corn-coloured wig with little plaits all over it. Oversized black sunglasses covered her creepy blue eyes—creepy to Doreen anyroad, but she was sure some people thought them beautiful, and she knew why they unnerved her so much, eyes from the past, eyes she'd rather forget. Cassie's baggy clothing (a grey tracksuit more in line with the young kids on the estate, not something Doreen thought was flattering at all) hung off her slender frame. If Cassie hadn't spoken, she wouldn't have known it was her. Was this how she dressed when she posted Doreen's wages through the letterbox late at night? Must be; she'd said she'd be in disguise.

"Right, yes, duck." Doreen stepped back. "I'm just writing *The Life* as it happens. I've got to get in touch with Sharon to see if she's aware of Karen's stall bookings for the February Fayre—you know, whether all the slots are filled. Should I take over that or leave it to Sharon?" She waited against the hallway wall while Cassie closed the door.

"Sharon can do it. I'll message her now. It'll give her something to focus on since her pal's copped it."

Cassie took her phone out and thumbed a message. Doreen thought about *The Life*, what she'd had to write in it versus what had really happened. Doreen had killed Karen by slicing her throat. No one must know. She couldn't bear for her Harry to find out. He'd stop seeing her, she was convinced of that.

"My crew have been to Karen's and emptied the place, so there's the computer Dad gave her going spare. I'll have it brought round here for you before they go off and dump her other shit." She sent another message. "There might be info on there about the Fayre. You can email it to Sharon."

"Oh, that'll be right handy, thanks. I've got an ancient laptop, takes forever to fire up, so having

Karen's proper computer will help. I'll buy a little desk and stick it in the spare room. Get one of them fancy chairs that help your back." Excited at the prospect of feeling important in her own little office, having a purpose in life other than working part-time at the betting shop and being Cassie's ears, Doreen wandered to the kitchen, wondering why on earth Cassie was in that get-up if she'd come to tell her something else needed putting in *The Life*. Assuming that was why she was here. It could be for any number of reasons since Doreen had shared the act of killing with the woman. They were allies now, Cassie having something concrete over Doreen, so perhaps this little scenario was for rules to be reestablished. The disguise was weird and unnecessary in Doreen's opinion, but there you go, what she thought didn't matter.

She prodded the kettle button and got busy with cups, choosing her best ones, remembering the day Cassie had come here to tell Doreen about her son, Richie, being sent to Marlene. Cassie had turned her nose up, and Doreen swore it was about her old bloody cups. She'd thought of her as a snooty bitch until recently.

Cassie walked in, sunglasses on top of her head and, instead of sitting at the table, she came to stand beside Doreen and propped her hip against a cupboard, her elbow on the worktop.

"Fuck me, you look fair worn out—if you don't mine me saying, like," Doreen said. "I'll admit I'm knackered, what with everything that went on—you know, Karen and Zhang Wei—but you need to get back to bed, lass."

"I *was* in bed, but Brenda phoned. Shit, Doreen, there's a mess I have to clean up, and I'm not sure I'm up to it. Mam said we have certain police in our pocket, but one of them has spilt some beans."

Bloody hell, Cassie unsure? Cassie talking to her about it and not Francis? That was a turn up for the books and no mistake, but Doreen was well glad about it. For this young woman to confide in her, well, it meant she trusted her, didn't it? That they were friends?

Or is this a test?

That threw cold water on her chuffed-as-fuck fire, and Doreen sobered. "You know you can talk to me and I won't blab, don't you? By killing Karen, I proved I'm with you, and I still am. Nowt will pass my lips, whatever you have to tell me. I'm not stupid enough to repeat what you say, unless you *tell* me to say it. Come on, get it out. What's the matter, duck?"

Cassie chewed on her bottom lip for a few seconds, tension radiating off her. "How much do you trust Lou?"

Christ, Doreen hadn't expected that. "She's champion, she is. Kept her mouth shut about certain things for years. We did something together then kept apart as much as we could, made out we'd gone in different directions in life so no one would suspect owt. Never once have I had any reason to doubt her."

Cassie sighed. Seemed to battle with whether to confess whatever was on her mind. "She killed Mr Plod after we'd done Karen over. I got home, and she had him in her fucking boot. She ran over him at the *factory*. His head popped and everything, bits of brain coming out."

Doreen's legs went all funny at the thought of that, plus… Oh, for the love of God. Lou had gone through with her mad idea after all. Why now, after all these years? She'd *promised* Doreen she wouldn't kill another person, said she'd behave, especially as Doreen had quizzed her about Superintendent Black. He'd fallen into the canal, well suss, and Lou had sworn it wasn't her pushing him in. Doreen had other ideas about that, but Lou had persisted with her story: Black had got drunk in The Donny, celebrating the end of a case, and wandered too close to the edge.

What the *hell* was she playing at?

"Um…right." Doreen staggered over to a chair and sat. She waved at the kettle. "Can you…? Flippin' 'eck, I feel sick."

Cassie poured steaming water into the cups, Doreen sucking in lungfuls of air to stop hyperventilating, telling herself she'd known this would happen, despite Lou's assurances, so why was she surprised?

Because she promised, and I thought she meant it.

Cassie sniffed. "That's not all. She got me and Mam roped into killing DCI Gorley. Well, ex-DCI, but you know what I mean. We went to see him this morning, and she used this thing on him she'd made. Wood with loads of nails sticking out. She stabbed his arm, cheek, and neck with it. I set fire to his shed on the allotment."

"Oh heck, Melinda, his wife, she won't keep her mouth shut if you're thinking of sending her one of them anonymous letters Lenny used to post to people after he'd offed someone. She's got a gob on her and then some. No matter whether you threaten her with disappearing, she'll shout it to the rooftops. She'll think Gorley's old colleagues will keep her safe from you."

Cassie poured milk. "I'm not contacting her. These copper deaths won't be publicly down to me, and that's why I'm here—along with talking about it to you, because Mam keeps telling me I have to stay strong, I needed to tell someone this is getting to me. How can I stay strong *all* the time? I've dealt with loads since Dad died, one thing after another, all big, all a lot to handle. I need you to write something in *The Life*, us being upset about the pig deaths, making it clear it isn't a Grafton job but not saying that outright."

Cassie finished making the drinks and brought them over. She passed Doreen hers and sat, sighing for so long Doreen had half a mind to brace herself for the girl passing out. Thankfully, Cassie was all right, so Doreen reached over and patted her hand.

"Lou told me about her plans years ago." Doreen's mind skipped back to a night in the pub, where they'd always said hello in passing but continued to keep their distance.

A short while after they'd broken the law, Doreen had moved out of their shared house, back to her childhood home, unable to stand what she'd done, what Lou had done. They'd been young, just eighteen and starting out alone, and it had all gone so horribly wrong.

"A couple of weeks after Jess was buried, we had a chat. I'd gone to the toilet in The Donny," she said, "and Lou was in there, a bit pissed up. Weaving, slurring, that sort of thing. She says to me, 'Dor, I'm going to be the piggy farmer'. And I thought that was well odd, seeing as she already was, what with Handel. Anyroad, she says, 'I'm going to kill them, all those who didn't save my Jess.' I told her not to, that messing with the police wasn't a good idea, and in the end, she swore to me she wouldn't. Then Superintendent Black drowned, and it just seemed too much of a coincidence for it not to have been her."

"Well, it must have got too much for her, because she followed Bob to the factory and ran him over on our property, for God's sake. Then she got Mam involved to get rid of the patrol car—close to the bloody squat."

"What's up with that?"

"Because I have Jason bastard Shepherd in there, haven't I. Got him to meet me last night after you'd gone home. I wanted him to admit he's been plotting to drug me and Mam, take over the patch. He didn't, so I shot him in the leg with my nail gun."

"Oh my sodding days." Doreen flapped a hand in front of her to cool her overheating face. "This is getting worse by the minute."

"Sorry to put all this on you, Dor, but I see you differently now, someone to turn to. Mam seems to think I can keep going without any emotions involved. Dad drummed it into me to keep myself hardened, and I was doing so well until Brenda rang me."

"What did *Brenda* want?"

"Sharon went round hers to say Bob and Gorley have been on the news. Some bloody copper leaked it to the press that Bob was missing in suspicious circumstances, yet Mam's police contact assured her he was hushing it up. I don't need fingers pointing our way. If coppers get sent to the factory, those forensic ones, and Marlene is tested…"

Doreen's head lightened, and she swallowed the saliva that flooded her mouth. "We don't need that." *She* didn't need that. She'd *been* there, in that effing side room with Marlene. Despite it being cleaned, the police might find something and… "Get rid of the leak." She couldn't believe she'd said that, especially with it being an officer and how she'd told Lou not to bother, but whoever was pouring oil on troubled waters, ready to light it then sit back and watch things burn, could cause a hell of a lot of hassle.

"I thought the same, I just needed a different perspective to see if it was the right thing to do." Cassie tugged at a plait. "Not the *right* thing, but you know what I mean."

"I don't like it any more than you do, but holes need to be plugged. Lenny would want you to do it."

"That's the problem half the time, Dor. I'm listening to Lenny's tune, even when he isn't alive to play it."

Chapter Thirteen

The Barrington Life – Your Weekly

FEBRUARY FAYRE AND POLICE NEWS

Doreen Prince – All Things Crime in our Time

Sharon Barnett – Chief Editor

FEBRUARY 2020

As you're probably aware by now, two police officers from our town have been on the news. PC Bob Holworth went missing on the road out to Worksop, his car seemingly vanishing, and ex-DCI Robin Gorley was burnt inside his shed. This is tragic, and Cassie has asked me to urge you all to be respectful of the coppers' families during this terrible time. Plus, she'd like us to send flowers to Robin's funeral, so a collection box will be on Sharon's face-painting stall at the Fayre. You can pop your small change in there, or even a fiver if you're feeling generous. Cassie has started the pot up with two hundred pounds. Francis has offered two thousand towards Robin's funeral costs. This will help Melinda Gorley out no end.

Now, while we're not fans of pigs, we don't condone one of them being torched, do we, so please, if you know owt, go to the police station and let them know. We live in sad times if people are resorting to murdering those who try to keep us safe, and as for Bob going walkabouts, that's really strange, concerning, so the sooner he comes home the better.

In other news, there's one stall left at the February Fayre this coming weekend (here's hoping the snow buggers off by then). As you know, proceeds from stall rentals are going to The Lenny Grafton Homeless Fund, a charity he set up to help those without housing in our town. There were still a couple of people on the streets as of this morning, no high-rise flats vacant for them, but Francis has paid for them to stay in Vera's B&B for now. A round of applause for that woman! She's already got the ball rolling on buying a couple of houses in Salway Street and turning them into bedsits for those who may find themselves without a place to call home in the future. Your money will help buy things like beds and such.

Also, don't forget to show up at the Fayre and enter the competition to win the all-inclusive holiday in Spain, donated by Cassie. Money raised by buying a ticket for a quid will also go to the homeless project.

I for one am proud to live on the Barrington with people like Francis and Cassie ensuring things get done. While Robin's death and Bob's disappearance are sad events, let's remember who we are and how we come together in a crisis. If we join as one, we can buy a carpet of flowers for Robin's graveside.

RIP.

Chapter Fourteen

*E*ighteen-year-old Doreen and Lou left The Donny, staggering along the road towards their home on the Barrington. They both lived in the same house, renting, sharing the kitchen and bathroom, their other housemate, Janine, away on holiday in Cornwall. It had felt so good to leave their respective *childhood places, branching out. Exciting, too. They were free of parental constraints, allowed to do whatever they liked, or it seemed that way anyroad.*

Summer had gifted the town with lots of sunshine this year, the air cooling—only a tad, mind—darkness fully eclipsing the lingering daylight. Doreen's nine-till-five job at the bookies had been a Godsend, coming right at the time she'd wanted to leave home. Frederick, the owner, was a friend of her dad's. Doreen wasn't daft. Dad would have put in a good word for her, then Frederick had made out he was casually chatting to her in the pub about needing an assistant, and: "Oh, so you need a job? Well then, that's settled. If you want it, that is."

Lou worked in Betty's Blooms, selling flowers, training on the job to become a florist. She had plans to run her own shop, so she'd said, and life was on the up. Doreen didn't like Betty; the battle-axe had told her off plenty of times over the years, like she had the bloody right. Doreen didn't usually carry slights over from childhood, but with Betty she made an exception. The older woman's tongue was as sharp as her pruning shears, and she had the thorns of the roses she sold an' all. Prickly cow.

They walked farther onto the estate, arms linked, Lou humming out of tune, Doreen recalling the conversation they'd had earlier about some bloke coming into Blooms, acting weird towards Lou. She'd said he kept buying bouquets then handing them back to her after paying, saying stuff like: "You deserve every flower in this shop. Fancy going for a drink?"

Lou always refused, said he gave her the creeps with his staring bright-blue eyes, and had even told Betty she felt harassed. The thing was, Betty said the man was only being romantic and Lou ought to be grateful she was getting any attention.

That wasn't right—rude, in fact, like Lou wasn't pretty enough to have a man treating her that way—

and Doreen had offered to go right up to Betty perched on the barstool sipping her Pernod and black, telling her to her face she should have her employee's bests interests at heart, but Lou wasn't having any of it. Instead, Doreen had given Betty evil stares a lot of the night, the hag giving them right back. God.

"I reckon that fella's got a screw loose," Doreen said now, her little handbag bumping her hip with each step. "You know, the one who buys you flowers."

Lou tripped on nowt, said, "Whoopsie daisy!", and giggled. "Yeah, he's a bit much. I've told him I don't want to go for a drink umpteen times now—like, a couple of times per visit—but he won't listen. Maybe I should tell him I fancy the pants off Joe Wilson. Then again, no. He might tell Joe, and I'd be right embarrassed, because Joe doesn't know how I feel."

It was simple to Doreen, the solution there if Lou had the balls to do it. "Why not just bite the bullet and *ask Joe out? If he says yes, at least you can tell the weirdo you're seeing someone. Who is he anyroad?"*

"That's the thing, I hadn't seen him before. He sounds like he's from Yorkshire." She paused walking and groaned. "For Pete's sake, I'm getting a bloody blister."

"You should have put plasters on like I said before we went out. New shoes, sore feet." Doreen shook her head. "Has he given you his name, the flower fella?"

Lou set off again, limping. "See, this is where it gets even stranger. He writes the cards himself, right in front of me on the counter, and signs them as 'S' with a kiss and a love heart. Like, the first time, what he'd written was romantic—because I thought it was for someone else."

That was coming on a tad strong. Who drew love hearts for strangers?

Doreen shuddered. "What did it say?"

Lou snorted. "You'll piss yourself. I'll never forget it: Roses are red. Violets are blue. I'm in your life. And I will have you."

"Err, okay… I don't find that funny. It's creepy."

"And he'd underlined 'will'. Like I said, I thought it was for someone else, but once he handed them over, that 'will' came off as sinister, like I had no choice but to go out with him in the end. Maybe I'm just being silly and he doesn't know how to chat girls up, so he thinks that's the way to go."

Doreen shivered, despite the muggy air. "Too right it's sinister. How many times has he been in since?"

"Five. Monday through to Friday this week."

"Bloody hell." Doreen couldn't imagine having someone being pushy with her like that. She had her eye on a bloke, but he was a bit of a lad, seemed to overly enjoy sowing his wild oats. She'd wait until he'd calmed down, then see if he wanted to date her.

Then again, did she want someone who was the town stud?

Lou swept her free hand through her hair. "And when I go for lunch at Sam's Café, you know the one, around the corner from work, I swear I feel someone watching me. It's that bad, I've been staying away from the window seats."

Doreen stopped and gaped at her friend. "Pack it in. That's seriously not right. I've got bloody goosebumps."

Lou shrugged, unlinking their arms and clutching Doreen's hand. "What do I do, though? I can't go to the police and say I think I'm being followed. I've got no proof, just a stupid feeling. I've never seen him around or owt, only ever in the flower shop."

"Next time he comes in, tell him if he doesn't stop it with the bouquets, you're calling the police, whether Betty Bitch likes it or not. It's harassment, that is."

"Betty would have a fit." Lou tugged Doreen back to walking.

"Fuck Betty. Stupid old goat."

Lou laughed. "She's okay, just sees 'S' as being passionate."

"I wonder what that stands for. Sam? Simon?"

"Spy."

"Yeah, or Stalker."

Lou squeezed Doreen's hand. "Don't. It's even weirder when I hear footsteps on my way home, but when I turn round, no one's there."

"What? Why didn't you say something? Or wait for me outside the betting shop and we walk home together? Jesus Christ, Lou."

"Keep your hair on. I'll do that from now onwards, okay?"

"You'd sodding better. We'll even get the bus if we have to. At least then if he gets on, we'll know it's him pissing about by walking behind you." But what if it

270

wasn't? What if someone else was doing it? "Is he the only one acting off?"

"Yeah. Everyone else is fine."

They'd reached the end of their street, and because there had been a lock-in at The Donny, it was late, and all the houses stood in darkness bar theirs, the streetlamps doing bugger all, dim as they were. They always left the outside light on beside the front door—Mam had given Doreen a long list of what to do, including looking out of the window before answering any knocks.

"You just don't know who's out there, Dor," she'd said.

Nervous now Lou had revealed some extra-creepy information, Doreen scanned the area, freaked out by the hedges at the bottoms of the gardens, all potential hiding places for Stalker. He could be crouching behind any one of them, ready to pounce on Lou and make her his. Doreen imagined him breathing faster because he'd spotted them.

"Bloody Nora, let's run." She legged it, dragging Lou along with her.

They reached their house, Doreen taking the lead at the gate, peering into the garden to check for shadowy shapes in the form of a flower-buying, poem-writing man. It was clear, the light just enough to see by, so she led her friend up the path, Lou taking her keys out of her bag, judging by the tinkle.

Inside, door shut, the chain in place, Doreen sighed with relief, feeling silly now they were safe. In the darkness of the hallway, the glow from outside coming in through the mottled glass panels, they stumbled and laughed while taking their high-heeled shoes off, Doreen banging her arse on the wall beside the telephone table.

"Fuck me, switch the light on, will you?" Lou asked. "I want to see the state of this blister."

Doreen hung her bag on the newel post then reached out and flicked the nearby switch, and the hallway flooded, the bulb so bright beneath its clear plastic shade that she couldn't see for a second or two. She blinked and turned to Lou, who stared ahead towards the kitchen, dropping her bag on the floor.

"What's the matter?" Trepidation seeped into Doreen's bones, sending her cold all over. If Lou was messing about, Doreen would soon have something to say about it, especially after the Stalker story.

"Someone just ran past the kitchen window from outside." Lou gripped the mahogany ball on top of the newel post, the ends of her fingers turning red from how hard she held it.

"Stop fucking around." Doreen's pulse banged in her neck vein, and she wanted to run, hide.

"I'm not."

Doreen let out a short scream and grabbed Lou's hand, taking her into the living room. They stood in the middle, clutching one another, Doreen's heart rate going crackers.

"What if it's Stalker?" she whispered. It could be, couldn't it? He could have definitely tailed Lou earlier after work and waited out there all night. The idea of that gave Doreen a jolt. He'd have to be well weird if he spent hours sitting on their wooden bench.

"Don't…" Lou's face paled.

"But it could be. You said you thought someone followed you home."

"Fucking hell… I'm scared, Dor."

"You and me both. Shall we phone the police?"

"And say what? I saw someone in the garden? I didn't even get a good look at them, just that it was a person."

"Was it like a man, though?"

"I think so, but it was too quick. Like, they ran."

A scraping sound, similar to branches on glass, had Doreen and Lou screeching, holding each other tighter, a lump barging into Doreen's throat. She dared to look over at the living room window. The thin curtains were drawn, a gap in the centre where they didn't quite meet, and the distinct slice of someone standing out there filled the space, one side of them lit up by the lamp.

"Don't look at the window." Doreen shook all over and made to guide Lou out of the room, back to the hallway where the phone sat on a table.

They didn't make it there.

Lou looked, trembling in Doreen's arms, and she sagged, her knees bending. "It's him. The flower man."

Pure terror pushed another small scream from Doreen. What to do? She tried to remember Mam's advice, but her mind was blank for a few seconds, then, "We're definitely ringing the police." She gripped Lou's hand and stomped them out of the room, aiming for the phone.

Glass shattered, fragments spewing inside to land on the lino tiles, showering onto Lou's handbag in chunks. Both of them screamed this time. A black-sleeved arm reached inside the hole in the front door, a gloved hand fumbling for the lock. Stalker snicked it down and pushed, but the chain prevented him from coming in. Doreen and Lou stood there, shocked, frozen, Doreen begging her legs to move, but they weren't listening, the ignorant bastards.

"Fuck off," Lou shouted. "We've phoned the police, so you'd better get lost."

Laughter entered the hole, low and sinister and so very wicked, and the hand moved downwards, patting for the chain. Lou snatched the phone up and placed the receiver to her ear. She turned to Doreen, her eyes going wide.

"There's no dial tone."

More laughter.

Had he cut the fucking wires?

"The kitchen," Doreen mouthed. She held Lou's upper arm and pulled her along the hallway, praying someone had heard them screaming, the glass breaking, and would come to see what was going on. That wasn't likely, though. They'd had a fair few parties since they'd moved in, and no one had nipped round to ask them to keep the noise down or complained to the landlord.

Jesus Christ…

In the kitchen, the door closed, Doreen snatched up a ladderback chair and propped it beneath the handle. It didn't look like it'd hold, it wasn't tall enough, but it would do for now, buying them time. Lou hammered on the adjoining right-hand wall in the dining area with her fists. Old Man Bodger wouldn't bloody hear it, he was deaf as a post, and his wife, Gladys, wasn't much better.

"The garden," Doreen said. "We'll climb over the fence and get Robby Denzil to help us."

Lou went to the back door, her fingers turning to sausages in her attempt to twist the key. She sobbed, panicking, staring at Lou with fear-crazed eyes, and it ramped up Doreen's anxiety. Key sorted, Lou wrenched at the handle, but the door remained closed.

"Undo the pissing bolts!" Doreen hissed.

Footsteps. The crunch of glass beneath shoe soles.

"He's coming!" Doreen wailed. "Fucking hell, fucking hell…"

She grabbed a carving knife from the drawer and faced the internal door, sick to her stomach that the night had turned into this. The handle moved down over the top of the chair, and she slapped her free palm over her mouth. The chair wobbled, pressure applied from the other side, and the sound of one of the bolts raking across the back door gave her hope.

Walking in reverse, the tip of the blade jabbed outwards, she stood by the window next to Lou, who'd *gone down on her haunches to yank the other bolt. It had always been sticky, and tonight it was no different.*

"It's bloody stuck," Lou said, breathless, a sob tagging onto the end of her words.

"Keep trying." Doreen's hands shook, the blade shivering.

The chair shifted forward in slow motion, then he crashed in, kicking at it so it skittered towards the dining table, time speeding up. Doreen screamed behind her hand, and Lou shot to standing, pawing the handle to open it, desperate for an escape route.

Stalker held a gun up, his gloved finger curled around the trigger. His eyes. God, they were such a startling blue she shuddered. They weren't natural.

"I wouldn't leave if I were you," he said, his Yorkshire accent thick. "Stay. With me."

Lou ignored him, so frantic she couldn't grasp the handle. Doreen, out of her mind with panic, rushed forward, and in the split second it took for her to get to him, she asked a God she'd never given a shit about to stop Stalker releasing the bullet. His eyes widened as she sank the blade in his stomach, and he dropped the gun, the sound of it hitting the lino weird—not a heavy thud, not loud. She pulled the knife out, jumping back, horrified by what she'd done—she hadn't intended on doing it, it'd just happened. But it would be classed as self-defence, so she wouldn't get in trouble, would she?

A terrible voice in her head whispered, "But it's still murder…" and she lurched into the table behind, staring at the blood on the knife, then back at him.

He clutched his stomach, blood pumping out, between and over his laced fingers, so much red. "Why don't you love me?" he said to Lou, whining. "Flowers are supposed to make you love me."

"Oh God, you fucking weirdo." Lou reversed to the wall, pressing her back to it. "Shit, Dor, what are we going to do?"

Doreen didn't think, just acted. She raced back up to him and sliced the knife across the side of his throat, blood spurting out and covering her face, hot, metallic. He sank to his knees then fell sideways, and she went down with him, watching the light fade from those wrong-kind-of-blue eyes that seemed to plead with her to help him. Doreen looked away, disgusted by the sight of him and the smell of copper, and gave the knife her attention, her hand, red splashes all over it, her wrist freckled, dots over the sleeve of her blouse.

"Shit. Shit!" Lou came over and peered down, a hand clamped to her chest. "He's still breathing. Oh God…" She held out her hand for the knife. "Give it to me."

Doreen passed it over, thinking Lou took it to stop her from slicing him again, but Lou knelt, held the handle in a double grip, and plunged the steel into his heart area. It stopped halfway up the blade, something resisting, so she leant all her weight on it until only the wooden handle was on show. She let go, watching him, her hands up as if that was proof she hadn't stabbed him.

Doreen, locked in this surreal world, scooted backwards on her arse, coming to a stop at the kicked-away dining chair, the end of a leg digging into her side. She stared across at Lou who'd bent her head so her ear was above Stalker's mouth.

"He's dead now." She turned to look at Doreen. "We're going to have to get rid of him."

"How?" Doreen swallowed bile then heaved, the stench of blood getting worse, clinging to the summer-thickened air. "We don't even have a car, and he's too heavy to carry far."

"Fuck."

Lou pulled the knife out and dropped it as though it burnt her hand. She came and sat beside Doreen, and they kept their attention on Stalker, Doreen convinced he'd get up any second, grab the gun, and shoot them.

Hot tears fell. Lou sobbed. They were in a right mess, no doubt about it, and with no one to turn to, no one they could tell, Shit Creek was the waterway they floated on.

Minutes passed, the only sounds their ragged breathing and the thud of Doreen's pulse filling her head. How had this happened? She couldn't process the events from when Lou had seen him run past the window to now. Her mind seemed to have erased it to protect her. Then it came rushing back, her brain regurgitating every terrible second.

Doreen whimpered.

"The well," Lou said.

And Doreen knew exactly what she meant. The one at the bottom of the garden, built with stone covered in moss from years of being outside, the little wooden roof a triangle, grey and faded from the sun. It had been there for over fifty years, according to the landlord, dried up, no use to anyone, just an ornament now.

"And did you know, it goes down about a hundred and thirty feet?" No, they hadn't known, and at the time hadn't given a fiddler's fuck, but now that information was gold.

"It's a long way down," Doreen said.

"So no one will know he's there."

"What if he starts to smell and people complain to the council?"

Lou went to chew on a thumbnail but stopped because of the blood on her skin. *"We'll wrap bin bags around him. Cut the bottoms off and down the sides so they're long bits of plastic."*

Doreen shifted her gaze to the gun. *"We'll need to get rid of that, too. And the knife."*

Lou got up on her knees and pushed herself to her feet. Doreen stared at the blister on her friend's heel. It had bled and appeared sore, but it was the least of their worries.

Lou stooped over the gun. "It looks like a toy. Plastic."

"Oh my God, what?"

Lou picked it up. "It is one." She stared at Doreen, her eyes filling again. "I can't believe this is happening. What if it gets out, what we did? What if someone sees us putting him in the well?"

"They won't. It's late. And no one will bloody know. I won't be saying owt. Will you?"

"God, no."

A surge of cover-this-shit-up gripped Doreen. "There you go then. Come on, we need to get this sorted."

It took ages to wrap Stalker, the blood creating a slippery environment, and at one point, with a layer on him, they pushed him to a cleaner part of the floor and mopped up, wrapped him again, then moved him to the washed area, repeating this until all the rubbish bags were used, all the packaging tape finished, and nearly all the blood scrubbed away. He was a mummy in black bandages, the brown tape crisscrossed. No matter how much Doreen told herself he was a rolled-up carpet, it still looked like a body.

He was heavy, cumbersome, but they managed, with Doreen gripping him beneath the armpits, praying her fingers didn't split the plastic, and Lou holding his ankles, to carry him into the garden. As Doreen walked backwards, she checked the windows of the houses, all in darkness, no one watching. Hefting him over the lip of the well seemed an impossible task. They raised his feet, and he shot away, Doreen counting the seconds for him to hit the bottom.

There were eighteen. Eighteen long ones, and a dull thud where he'd landed. The smell Lou had mentioned bothered Doreen—a rotting corpse, the reek coming through any possible gaps in his shroud—and she had an idea what to do. Back in the house, she shut the door and plonked onto a chair. Lou stripped out of her clothes. Ran the tap with cold water, filling the sink.

"We'll do the garden up," Doreen said. "Order a load of bags of peat to be delivered tomorrow afternoon. Enough so we can tip some into the well and it'll cover him. That should help with the smell. We'll keep a bag or two, then turn the borders over, plant some flowers, and sprinkle peat on top so it looks to Janice when she comes back that we were busy while she was gone. Any nosy neighbours peering across at the garden won't think twice about the peat delivery then either."

"That's going to cost a lot. How much do you think we need to cover him? I don't get paid that much, remember." Lou put her dress in the sink. "Give me your clothes."

Doreen got up and tugged her shirt and blouse off, handing them to Lou. A line of blood had splashed on the window and part of the sill from where she'd arced the knife after slicing his neck. She'd clean it but would always see it, even when it was gone. "I've got some savings. Mam gave me spare money. And as for the bags, say twenty? That haberdasher fella will drop it round, you know, the one who owns that shop in town. We can get him to carry it into the garden, and we'll chat to him, tell him we're making it nice, like."

Lou prodded Doreen's clothes beneath the water, which turned pink. Doreen's face was tight from the dried blood on her skin, and she stood there in her bra and knickers, shivering despite it being summer.

"I need a bath," she said, "but we should clean up even more first, use bleach, and that front door needs cardboard over it until we can get someone to fix it. Maybe the peat bloke will do it. We'll say we had to break in because we forgot our keys."

Lou nodded. "I'll get in the bath after you, so don't stay in for ages else the water will get cold."

What a weird thing to think about at a time like this.

Lou gave a sad smile. "This is our secret forever?"

Doreen nodded. "Forever."

Chapter Fifteen

The snow had stopped falling around ten this morning, and a thaw had steadily crept in over the course of the day, grass valiantly poking through on some of the verges, a gulley made on pavements, tarmac on show, although it appeared shiny, coated with sparkling ice—watch your step or you'd go arse over tit.

On the breakfast news, his hair gelled back and a veneer smile covering the fact he'd probably been up since three a.m. for work, the weatherman had said it'd most likely be gone soon, all that snow, which would make for a boggy Sculptor's Field once everyone trampled over it at the weekend, unless a frost hardened it. Wellies, Lou would need those. She was doing the pie and jam stall. Thank goodness the jam was already made, but she'd still need to bake the pies.

The February Fayre was the last thing on her mind at the minute, though. She stood beside Francis in the darkness of the yard behind The Lion's Head, Cassie on Francis' left. It was weird being on the Moor estate, as if they weren't as safe as they'd be on the Barrington. That made sense, as they knew every road and pathway on their patch, but the Moor, she'd only been there once or twice to visit an old school friend, and that had been a month or so after the Stalker business.

She hadn't been tempted to tell Josephine about it, the promise she'd made to Doreen as strong as ever. The horror of it had taken two weeks to fade a little, Lou's terrible dreams lessening, her fear of being caught diminishing somewhat, although it was all still there, lurking in the dark recesses inside her, ready to come out when she wasn't expecting it. Sleep and a bad situation had an unspoken agreement: to torment you with whatever happened, chasing you in your nightmares, no matter how much time had passed.

Doreen hadn't been able to handle staying at the house, saying the garden gave her the willies every time she glanced out there or pegged her washing on the line. She imagined Stalker moaning from the bottom of the well, or whispering to her at night, and had convinced herself Robby Denzil had watched them commit murder and would grass them up, even though his house had been in darkness and he hadn't said owt or acted funny when they'd seen him two days later. She'd moved back home to her mam's. Lou had stayed, getting herself accustomed to their final agreement on the day Doreen had walked out: they'd avoid each other as much as possible, so they weren't tempted to discuss it and risk being overheard, but remain friends deep down. How could they *not* be friends when joined by the common thread of murder? Doreen had stabbed him in the stomach and sliced his throat to protect them, and Lou would never forget that.

To appear 'normal', she'd got herself caught up the flurry of a bubbly new housemate, Deborah, moving in. She'd hid a grimace when Deb—"I prefer being called that, Deborah is so formal…"—pushed open the kitchen window one night, her hand on where the blood had spattered. Janice hadn't spotted owt amiss when she'd got back from her holiday, but Doreen was convinced she would. Janice was a strict cleaner and would spy even a tiny drop of blood. She'd queried the missing knife, though, and Lou had lied: "No idea where it's gone, love, sorry."

That added to the fear.

Lou blinked herself out of the past and focused on tonight. Cassie had brought a map of the Moor up on her laptop earlier, and they'd studied their entry and exit routes, any possible alternatives if things went wrong. Cassie had grumbled that she didn't know where all the CCTV cameras were, and wasn't that just a kick in the teeth, then said they'd have to pray they didn't get clocked. She'd sounded arsey, like Lou's quest was a pain in her rear end and she didn't want owt to do with it.

Talk about rude.

I bet Jess wouldn't treat me like that.

Lou didn't see the problem, CCTV or not. They had another stolen car, false plates, and balaclavas, so what did it matter whether they were caught on camera? Once they got back onto the Barrington, Cassie could lose them in the maze of streets easily, then take the car to the scrappy bloke, switch into hers, and be done with it.

Cassie had provided black boilersuits to put on over their clothes, and along with leather gloves, plus the wool covering Lou's face, she was sweating buckets. A thrill went through her at imagining Joe thinking she was curled up on

Francis' sofa, wine in hand, all of them chatting, then she bumped down to earth with guilt paying her a nasty unwanted visit. She shouldn't delight in deceiving him tonight, but hadn't she done that for the whole of their relationship, minus the revelling in it? If he knew she'd stabbed Stalker in the heart and pushed him down a bloody well, and nudged Superintendent Black into the canal when she'd followed him from The Donny that time, he'd be devastated, not only because of the deception but he'd ask himself who the chuff he'd married—and whether he should tell the police about her.

Don't think about it. Get these coppers killed and that's an end to it.

It had to be the end. She couldn't continue in this way. Lying to Joe…should she confess her past and what she'd done recently? Would he leave her or understand why she'd done it? He was a kind man, the best, and didn't deserve a liar for a wife.

Francis' arm brushed Lou's, reminding her she wasn't alone. Lou often went inside her head, examining her memories, trying not to acknowledge how her warped brain strung together completely unconnected events. Like Janice going to Cornwall, so Lou had sent Jess there to keep her safe, the same as Janice had been safe from having owt to do with the murder of the creepy flower man. Doreen had confessed once, during a rare chat in the market, that Cassie's eyes gave her the creeps because they were the same shade as his. Maybe Lou wasn't so weird after all and everyone's brain worked the same way, joining events by association.

"What's taking them so long?" Cassie whispered.

Still grouchy then.

Upon arrival, headlights off, Cassie had reversed the car between the yard's high brick wall and a stack of empty beer barrels, muttering that the car had better not be seen or there'd be trouble.

"Creep up the side of the pub and look through the window to see if Knight and Codderidge are inside yet—and stay back in the dark," Cassie had said.

As if Lou wouldn't know that. As if she'd *let* people see her in a fucking balaclava.

"I wasn't born yesterday," Lou had sniped back and sidled along the wall, making a show of doing it right.

They were sitting at a table, those pigs, plates of food piled high—*carb overload, you greedy bastards*—a pint of lager for Knight, something with Coke, ice, and a slice for Codderidge. The pair of them lived on the Barrington so must come to the Moor thinking they wouldn't be spotted by their other halves and had done this for years. She didn't know how someone hadn't grassed them up yet, but then again, people around here would think it was two coppers chatting shit after work and take no notice, wouldn't they.

Lou knew about the affair from an early evening one winter. She'd gone to The Lion's Head to spy years ago, Joe busy at the farm fixing a broken fence at the edge of the property, and she'd gone out under the guise of having one of her 'drives'. She'd spied on them through that very side window, then, once they'd got up to leave, she'd pressed herself into the darkness, expecting them to walk past the turning into the yard, but they'd come towards her instead, Knight shoving Codderidge against the wall and snogging her, then they'd gone into the yard proper, hand in hand, Lou swearing they'd spot her any second.

If they were good coppers, they would, but look how they didn't even find my Jess.

Immobile, she'd watched them get up to certain things beside a large wheelie bin close to the back of the pub, the light from an upstairs window shining down enough that she got the gist—the same light that was on now—showcasing hands and fumbles and kisses and laughter. And grunts. She'd wanted to be sick but had to wait until they'd left. How could they *do* that when her child was dead? How could they giggle and create such *appalling* sounds? Didn't they *care*?

She'd returned another night, same time, different week, and they'd been at it like rabbits again. A nudge in the right direction from her sent gossips nattering in The Donny, letting her know the affair had been going on for years, and nowt was done about it because: "It isn't any of my business where he pokes his sausage stick, duck."

Lou shivered. Hoped they'd come out soon so they could get on with it and kill the fuckers. Her nail weapon was in place, a new best friend on her steady hand, even snugger because of the glove.

Cassie and Francis had baseball bats.

Lou thought about any evidence left behind from them, but that should be minimal. They were covered up well, and the landlord must have cleared the snow out here for the deliveries, so no tyre tracks or footprints for other piggies to nose at once the bodies were discovered.

The back door opened, one used by smokers, and some round-as-a-ball fella emerged, laughter and music from the pub floating out behind him, telling of lives lived without unhappiness in them, or maybe they laughed because, well, if you didn't, you'd go mad.

Like me.

He sparked up, took a drag, the end of his cigarette glowing orange. Lou swore the tension around her pressed close, a tangible thing. Cassie had sewn the mouth holes up in the balaclavas, but Lou was paranoid their clouds of breath would give her away. Her skin was wet around her lips, on her chin, and she had the urge to wipe it, but she couldn't move else she risked them being spotted.

A few more drags, then his phone rang. Lou jumped at the loud tone, her chest seeming to hollow from her heart beating so wildly, and she reminded herself to keep calm. Her body trembled, and she couldn't stop it. Was this a portent? Were they going to get caught? Was this a sign to tell them to abandon the job?

The fella dug his phone out of his jeans pocket and swiped the screen, the light bringing his face into sharp focus. Bushy beard. A squished nose. Thick lips. Ruddy skin. He scuffed the concrete with his boot, and a small stone skittered. "Yeah? At the pub… I've only had one pint… *Tsk*. I'll come home now, all right?"

Someone wasn't happy their bloke was in the boozer.

He stuffed his phone away. "Can't bleedin' go anywhere on my own these days." He traipsed off down the side of the building, coughing.

That bloody door would pose a problem in other circumstances, but Cassie had a metre-long piece of wood to prop beneath the handle, preventing anyone coming out once their targets were in place.

She'd thought of everything.

It reminded her of when Doreen had put that chair beneath the handle in their kitchen. This time, though, the wood would actually do something worthwhile.

At her thought of killing, Lou's heart sped up, and she blew out a breath.

"How long does it take to eat pie and fucking chips?" Cassie muttered.

"Quiet," Francis warned.

Lou wanted to answer, griping at Cassie to follow her own bloody rules and shut her gob. Instead, she stared at the pub and went through their plan. They'd pull this off. They had to.

Time dragged. Cassie and Francis were true pros—they stood still, waiting, waiting, while Lou fidgeted. They even breathed quietly, while Lou panted. What must they look like, three figures in the dark against the wall, masks on, weapons in hand? Part of Lou couldn't believe she was doing this, but the other...it couldn't wait to get started.

More time passed. What if Knight and Codderidge had been called away on a case? Had they abandoned their dinner to run off and help someone else, giving *them* their full attention, the opposite of what they'd done for Jess?

Stop winding yourself up.

The door opened, and out they tumbled, the pervy pair, Amy Winehouse singing about a woman called Valerie in the background. Lou stiffened, so *angry* at the sight of them, and she had the stupid urge to rush them, stab the shit out of their faces, obliterating those looks of years ago, the pity, the 'we'd love to keep looking for your daughter, but *he* won't let us'.

Lies. All lies.

Knight led Codderidge to their usual tryst spot, and this was where Lou had winced when Cassie had laid out the plan. They had to *stand* there and let them get into it, trousers down at his ankles, then strike. It made sense, but having to hear them doing it again had Lou's guts rolling. She glared over at the coppers who were partial shadows, the light from the window sending the blackness grey where they were, perhaps a dimmer bulb than before, but it was enough to differentiate the shapes and work out what they were.

"God, I can't get enough of you," Knight said.

God, I can't wait to rip your fucking face off.

Lou gritted her teeth and flexed her fingers beneath the weapon across her knuckles. Francis' breathing got faster, and Lou could only hope it wasn't because of what those two were doing, but anger on Lou's behalf that the pigs acted as if they didn't have a care in the world when Jess was likely bones in that coffin by now—

no, she's on the beach; she's playing with her pink bucket.

—forgotten, her cute little face but a memory to them, one they couldn't remember because they'd filed her away, case closed, now move on.

A strange growl echoed, and Lou's disgust level went up a notch until Francis elbowed her and Lou realised it was coming out of her own mouth. Pain, that was what it sounded like, a terrible expression of the grief she still experienced.

Knight's trousers dropped, his pasty skin two slim trunks in the gloom. Lou gagged, sweat breaking out beneath the mask, and while Knight did all the moves associated with *that*, Cassie crept away, a bat in one hand, the wood plank in the other.

Game on.

Chapter Sixteen

T he coppers were so caught up in what they were doing, they didn't stop to look over and spot Cassie wedging the length of wood beneath the door handle, nor did they perk up at the soft scrape of it on the ground.

Her nerves were serrated being so close to the light coming from a top window—and she hated doing business outside the Barrington—but if this stopped Lou from taking matters into her own hands again, murder had to be done. The woman was seriously doing her head in, butting in during the planning phase this afternoon and generally grumping about the decisions.

"*Who* knows how these things work?" Cassie had shouted. "*Me and Mam*, not you!"

Lou had narrowed her eyes at her and sulked.

With no snow in the yard, it made things easier, although Cassie had cringed in case the shagging pigs had copped on to her footsteps on the way over to the pub. She held her breath and sidled to the wheelie bin, gasps from Codderidge infecting the air. Cassie raised her bat, stepped out behind Knight, prayed Mam was already coming out of her hiding place, and brought the weapon down on the back of his head. He fell to his knees, and there was a millisecond where Cassie stared at Codderidge's shadowed face, then Mam's bat connected with the copper's forehead.

With both of them on the ground, Cassie managed to drag a moaning Knight and dropped him away from the bin. Lou swept in and went straight for Codderidge, who groaned and possibly held a hand up to her face, difficult to tell, the side of the extra-large bin blocking the light. The nail weapon launched, Lou grunted, then stepped back, only to swing her arm in a downwards arc and stab Codderidge in the top of the head. Knight shifted, so Mam walloped him again, probably on the leg, and he cried out.

It was frustrating doing this in the dark. Cassie couldn't properly see what either of her partners in crime were doing, their figures murky, darting about around Knight. If they didn't need to be careful about being spotted, she'd have put on her night-vision goggles with the head torch on the front.

"You fucking piece of pig-shit scum bastard," Lou said quietly. "Let's see how *you* like dying."

A sickening thud followed by a wet squelch, and Cassie had an idea Lou had stabbed him in the throat. It had worked for Gorley, so why not? Movement to Cassie's left had her spinning that way, adrenaline pumping. Codderidge was getting up, moaning and crying.

"Shut up," Cassie warned her.

Lou barrelled into Cassie, sending her shifting to the side, and a blur of ghost-like shadows danced, the noises of boots scuffing the ground and strange growls creating a disturbance they didn't need. Too disorientated to scream, Codderidge mumbled incoherently, and Lou lugged her out from beside the bin. She attacked her face, her arm lashing out violently, swipe after swipe. Cassie turned to look for Mam, who crouched beside Knight.

"This one's gone," Mam said and stood.

So Lou's weapon had finished him off.

Animal sounds came out of Lou, who was going to town on her victim, possessed, seemingly unable to stop. Cassie gripped the back of Lou's boilersuit and tried hauling her away, but the silly cow was too frenzied, too strong with anger. She'd fuck this right up if she wasn't careful. There wasn't enough *time* to have the luxury of wrecking Codderidge's face.

"Mam," Cassie whispered. "Help me get her off."

Mam used her bat and hit Lou's weapon arm enough to hurt but not to break any bones. Lou spun around, the nail block raised, stepping farther into the edge of the light. One side of the balaclava was somewhat visible. Blood that appeared black had splashed onto the skin around Lou's eye.

"Don't you fucking *dare* come at me with that," Mam said. "Finish her off, for God's sake. We need to go."

Cassie glanced over at the door. It wouldn't be long, and someone would try to leave so they could have a fag, and shit would hit the fan once they couldn't get outside. She turned to Lou, who'd moved back to a silent Codderidge, and Cassie's monster smiled as the twenty-three nails sank into the officer's neck.

Coffee cake and champagne were an odd combination, the different tastes creating a revolution on Cassie's tongue, both fighting to win the war. She abandoned the champagne—she'd be driving again anyroad—and finished the cake, wishing she didn't have to go to the squat and burn the boilersuits, balaclavas, and gloves, not to mention the piece of wood and the baseball bats (the latter with blood on them, Mam's coated more than Cassie's from where she'd staved the front of Knight's head in, and Lou had sawn them into smaller pieces in the shed not five minutes after they'd got back). Cassie had run the saw through the dishwasher because of the blood transfer on the teeth.

She'd managed another nap prior to Lou arriving after dinner but was lethargic from not only being tired but the drab and heavy feeling she always got once an adrenaline rush wore off. She was in need of a full night's sleep, but that wasn't on the agenda just yet.

Lou's eyes had that mad gleam in them, and she necked back her champers. "Jess is happy."

Cassie didn't know what to say so glanced at Mam who shrugged.

"She's giggling like she did in Gorley's shed." Lou poured more alcohol. "Everything's better now."

"Good," Mam said. "You can finally move on."

"Never. Not when you have a stalker on your mind."

Cassie slumped. For fuck's *sake*, was there *more* to deal with? Were they going to have to hold Lou's hand *again*? "Stalker?"

Lou's eyes deadened. "What?"

Mam frowned. "You said you had a stalker."

"Did I?" Lou blushed and darted her eyes left then right. "Um, well, I don't know why I said that. Just ignore me." She gulped more champagne, flustered, appearing guilty.

Why?

Mam didn't look too honest either, the dawning of a memory transferring to her face in the form of a frown.

Cassie swallowed the last piece of her cake and stood. That little conversation had unsettled and annoyed her. Lou might be Mam's friend, but she was proving to be a pest they didn't need. Why mention a stalker if she didn't have one? What did Mam know that Cassie didn't? Who was the stalker?

Fuck it. If those to want to hide shit, they can get on with it. "I'm going to the squat."

The black bag of clothes and wood sat by the front door (they'd all stripped and showered). Lou had borrowed some of Mam's leggings and a top, just in case any blood had seeped through her boilersuit, and she'd said she'd be telling Joe she'd got wet by lying in the back garden and creating an angel in the snow for Jess, drunkenness pushing her to do it. Personally, Cassie felt that particular lie was sick, but Lou had smiled, her eyes vacant where she was off in her head again. How she'd explain not getting her clothes back was anyone's guess, but like Cassie had already thought, they couldn't help the nutbag with everything.

"So soon?" Mam asked.

"Yes, I need some fresh air." What Cassie didn't say was: *I'm sick of Lou, can't stand to look at her. She's changed, getting worse. Needs help.* "Don't wait up."

Depending on how she felt once the cold had woken her up again, she might kill Jason, get him sorted and out of her hair once and for all. Then, if the residents behaved, she might have a few days where nowt happened.

That's a joke.

With the February Fayre coming up, a large crowd forming, there was bound to be some aggro she'd need to step in to break up. Alcohol pushed people to do stupid things, and arguments would break out, slights from years ago dredged up:

What about that time you spilt beer on me in The Donny?

What? That was yonks ago. What about when you punched my kid for picking one of your missus' flowers?

Fuck me, talk about holding a grudge.

Says you who's still naffed off about a fucking pint. I bought you another one, didn't I?

I think you'll find you didn't, pal.

Must be someone else I'm thinking of then.

She left the kitchen, grabbed the clothes bag, and went out to the car. The scrappy was dealing with the other one used tonight, stolen for her by her trusty little thief, and she'd slipped him and the scrappy a bonus. Money was a surefire way to buy silence, but she didn't *need* to hand them extra: the men had never given her any reason to question or mistrust them. She'd done it out of appreciation.

The drive to the squat was easier than before, the middle of the road clear of snow, although the verges and surrounding fields still had a quilt over them, and some white clung to hedge tops in marshmallow clumps. She had her weapon in her briefcase in the boot and considered using it on Jason again to reopen all those hardened face wounds, but something else came to mind to finish him off, and that was not only more satisfying but in tune with farming the piggies out.

Jason was a pig, just a different kind. A traitor, someone who'd admitted what he'd planned, therefore she had proof. What did Lou have except suspicions that the officers hadn't tried hard enough to find Jess? Lou had based this mission on her feelings, on what she *thought* the police had been thinking, and Cassie now realised she should never have agreed to join the bacon hunt.

She'd admit that Mam backing Lou up had swayed her, plus Mam would have helped her whether Cassie was in on it or not. Funny how your parent still influenced you, regardless of whether you were an adult. She'd trusted Mam's judgement, but it had been foolhardy to put themselves in danger, especially on the Moor. While she was confident the car, the false plates, and their disguises would make things incredibly difficult for the police to track them, there was always the chance they'd get caught.

Not every pig was in their pay.

She sighed and turned into the squat's driveway, again parking around the back. The snow hadn't thinned out here, the front and rear gardens as thick as they'd been before, although a trodden-down patch by the kitchen door proved Jimmy had been coming out for his ciggies, hopefully before she'd warned him to remain inside. Perhaps by some unconscious decision, he hadn't tossed the butts. In the light of her headlamps, no telltale signs of them spearing holes in the snow were evident.

She'd made the right choice choosing him, just needed to up his confidence, get him to believe in himself. And maybe he'd eventually become used to violence.

Cassie: *I'm here.*

Jimmy: *Okay. Kitchen again.*

She got out and collected what she needed from the boot. Checking the area, she walked down the side of the building, glad she'd put her boots on. The top layer of snow crackled then crumped beneath her feet as she flattened it, and it reminded her of Dad taking her up a big hill once, and they'd rolled down the snow to the bottom.

Her eyes stung. Was Yenay having similar thoughts, memories colliding in her head of Zhang Wei and the fun they must have had, what they could *still* have had if Mam hadn't shot him, if he hadn't pushed it and found himself at the end of Cassie's and her mother's frayed tethers?

I can't change it. Move on.

She entered the squat and locked up behind her, dumping one item in the living room on the bookshelf, pausing at the eerie sensation she was being watched. Cassie turned to the back wall. Jason was awake, and he stared at her, so still she thought he was dead. She walked over to him and kicked his nailed leg.

He screamed.

Not dead then.

She strutted out, closing the door and taking the black bag into the kitchen. Jimmy stood by the kettle again, a cup of something already made, an empty mug beside it, one he must have got out when she'd texted. A good man, was Jimmy.

"You have no idea how much I need that drink," she said and moved to the furnace. Repeating her actions like she had with Bob's clothes, she set about feeding the fire.

"Bad day?" he asked.

"Depends on your perspective. Some would say it was a brilliant day, things getting done. Me? Not so sure." She couldn't divulge more than that. Wished she had a friend she could trust so much that she could chat about her weird life, although Doreen was fast becoming someone she wanted to confide in. Maybe Jimmy would become one of those people, too.

"Want to talk?" He smiled.

"I'd love to, but while I trust you, I don't trust you enough."

"I get it."

She appreciated him not pushing it, either because he was too scared to, or he was genuinely not that kind of bloke.

"I won't let you down," he said. "I'll prove it an' all."

"It'll take time." She threw the last piece of wood in the flames.

"Yeah."

She closed the furnace door, hadn't cared whether Jimmy copped any eyeful. Before, she'd wanted to hide Bob's uniform, needing to keep Mr Plod's death quiet, but now…now she'd made the decision it was okay to have the bodies out in the open, and a twinge of regret tweaked in her chest.

Too late to turn the clock back.

"Own your mistakes," Dad whispered in her head.

What, like you owned yours? Like fuck, did you. You hid them from us.

She huffed at that, the cheek of it, and Jimmy stared at her as if he'd done something wrong, worrying a pimple with his fingertip.

"It's not you I'm snorting about, just something I was thinking of." She took the coffee from him, leaning on one of the cupboards. Funny how she'd picked the same spot to stand as before. Mind, there weren't many places she could rest her backside in this place. Mam had an old table and chair set in the garage, a plastic one for the patio. Maybe Cassie would bring them here.

Jimmy picked the top off of a spot and winced.

Cassie had to say something. "The last thing I want to do is offend you, because you're a decent bloke, but I'm saying this out of concern. Can't you go to the doctor about those? It seems more of a problem than general acne. Get some steroid cream or whatever for them."

Jimmy seemed to have a light-bulb moment. "I didn't think of that."

"Get it sorted. You'll feel better once you have." She patted his shoulder, the only sign of affection she was prepared to give, plus her old self felt guilty for bringing up something he was clearly embarrassed about. Once his face was healed, she reckoned his self-confidence would grow. She needed him stronger, with a bit of backbone to him. "How's *he* been?" She jerked her head in the direction of the living room, getting ready for the bad—"good," her monster whispered—stuff.

"Fucking weird." Jimmy turned his back to the blind-down window, folded his arms, and leant on the unit beside the gap where a white-goods appliance would have stood. "He woke up and just stared. Like, I know he can't help it because of what you did to his eyelids, but Christ, it freaked me out. That's why I came in here to make a cuppa, to get away from him. There's only so long I can stand looking at him, being in the same room as him."

I know the feeling. It was the same with Lou.

"And," Jimmy went on, "to think I was scared of him that night you came to my flat. He showed me his gun, you know; it was in a holster. Now, he's just pitiful, no one to be frightened of at all.

The tables have turned, because now *I'm* the one with the gun."

Was Jimmy saying he was glad he was the scary one now? It sounded promising. She'd make a hardman out of him yet.

Cassie got a flash of Jason's ruined face in her mind. "Hmm, he is a bit of a state, and I told him off about the gun business, he should never have done that. Anyroad, I've decided he'll be dead tonight, so you won't have to be here anymore. Well, not once we've removed the body."

Jimmy's eyes widened, and he opened his mouth to speak, but Cassie got there first.

"Don't worry. I'll treat this as if you've killed him and give you the twenty grand."

"Fuck me."

"Much as I like you, Jim, no thanks."

He laughed and reached for his drink. "I didn't mean… Shirl would kill me if I touched you like that."

"So would I."

They chuckled for a bit, and it was good to release some tension, good he'd taken what she'd said as banter. Laughter was apparently the best medicine, and whoever had originally said it, they could be onto something. Cassie didn't have much to laugh about, though, or maybe she wasn't looking hard enough, *trying* hard enough to find the bright spots in life. How could she when murder and treachery were all around her, taking up her time?

Drink finished, she sighed. "Right, we'd best be getting on then. Prepare yourself, because this won't be pretty. Not only will you watch me kill him, but you'll be coming to see Marlene with me. And if you breathe a word about who she is, I'll give you to her." How quickly she'd banished the bonhomie, but Jimmy needed to know she was serious.

"I won't say owt," he stuttered. "I swear it."

She smiled again, nicely, none of that tight-lipped rubbish. "I wouldn't either if I knew I was getting twenty K, tax free."

Chapter Seventeen

Forty-five-year-old DI Gary Branding stood in the light from three halogens on tall stands placed around The Lion's Head yard. Forensics milled about doing their thing, white-suited and sombre, hoods up, masks on, booties covering their shoes. Pale spectres, that was what they looked like, sent to haunt the crime scene, searching for clues to bring the killer to justice. Another team were still at the allotment, working beneath the cover of a white tent, sifting through the burnt remains, although Gorley's husk of a body had been removed.

A tent was in the process of being set up here, too, and another one would follow, shielding the bodies from any snow should it come down, but most importantly, anyone who gawped out of the pub's rear windows—they were still being questioned by PCs and DC Strong in the bar area, but it wasn't uncommon for a nosy wanker to drift away from distracted officers, on the guise of using the toilet, to have a butcher's. The side driveway had been cordoned off, blocking entry, and a PC stood there with the log for signing in and out of the scene.

He silently thanked the landlord for clearing the yard of snow. The logistics involved in preserving the scene had it been covered in white was something Gary didn't want to think about.

It could be any one of the murder situations he'd found himself in over the years. Except it wasn't. The whole thing had an extra layer of iffy, and he'd need to have his wits about him to get through it—and he'd have sleepless nights worrying whether he'd missed owt. He was the appointed Senior Investigating Officer, thank God, and would be on hand to divert his colleagues' attention away from things they shouldn't be aware of if the need arose, but he couldn't keep an eye on them all the time, couldn't know every piece of evidence written in their notebooks until the full reports came through. And then? He could hardly tell them to change their findings, exposing himself as bent, which meant he'd have to chat to the team in incident room briefings so he could steer those clues in another direction prior to reports being written: away from the truth.

The Dracula-lookalike pathologist, Evan Merton, crouched beside the male victim, whose grey trousers and red boxers bunched around his ankles. Male victim—Gary had to think of him as that while studying him in order to remain objective; just a body, no one in particular. He'd done the same at Gorley's scene, finding it difficult to hold back emotions regarding his ex-superior, who'd been a good friend, stuffing his feelings deep down, bringing his detective heart into play—and his criminal one now he worked for Francis and Cassie.

Two of their own, DC Simon Knight and DS Lisa Codderidge, had been murdered a few metres away from the pub. Had this been on the

Barrington, he'd suspect people in the boozer had been warned to keep their mouths shut, to lie, too scared to do otherwise, but this was the Moor estate. Although… Codderidge's face was a bloody, ripped-up mess, so this could be Cassie's doing, using her barbs. Why would she kill more officers, though? *If* she'd killed Bob. Francis hadn't said whether the man was dead, hadn't warned him of owt like this going down either, and he'd like to think she would have, seeing as she'd employed him to cover up any dirty work. All she'd spoken to him about was Bob, that he was 'missing', but that implied death, didn't it? With Gorley and these two now dead, it was looking like a connection stared him in the face, one he'd have to snuff out.

How the fuck would he get the Graftons out of this one if they'd had a hand in it? Maybe she hadn't told him on purpose. His reactions had been genuine; fellow officers wouldn't suspect him.

Clever bitch.

He didn't feel any guilt whatsoever about being in their pay—he couldn't, not with the goings-on at his house. Gorley had been in with Lenny, Gary knew that for a fact, the secret whispered by the then DCI one night in The Donny, and Gary had wanted that for himself, *needed* it. His wages hadn't stretched once his wife, Trish, had got ill with a muscular disease and had to give up her job, but *he'd* been stretched, having to work overtime while worrying about not being home enough to watch over her. Their daughter had stepped up to the plate, but she shouldn't have to. With Francis giving him ten grand for Bob, plus a so far unspecified amount each week from now on, he could employ a freelance carer, someone to nip in two or three times a day to see how Trish was doing, and to sit with her, put her to bed on those evenings he couldn't leave the station on time—or like tonight, where he'd gone home but had to come out again to *this* mess, leaving Trish a captive to their mattress.

Gary, in protective clothing himself, approached Evan, who'd moved on to the female victim. And it hit him then, that while it sounded fantastical, these two murders might not be connected to Gorley and Bob. The first two could be unrelated—Bob had pissed the Graftons off, for whatever reason, and Gorley had placed something too close to his gas fire and died.

No, the latter wasn't right, not that anyone else knew that. Just in case it was a Grafton hit, Gary, being the first on scene after the firefighters, had spotted a padlock in the ashes, in the locked position, and carefully, with his back to the fire crew, he'd swiped it up, placing it in his coat pocket. If it had been on the outside of the shed door, it would point to murder, and he for one didn't want to be the SIO on *that* situation (but he was, to cover for Francis). The post-mortem results hadn't come back for Gorley yet, it was perhaps too soon, and Gary prayed the bloke had just been burnt and there were no signs of foul play.

This scene... Had one of their spouses finally found out about the years-long affair, following them? Had they seen what was so obviously happening, going off on one? With nowt here that could have been used as a weapon, they had to have brought one—or two—with them, so it was premeditated, a conscious decision to harm. This had all the signs of a rage attack, personal, what with the state of the woman's face. Someone had gone to town on it, blood spatter everywhere, her

342

cheeks ripped, one of her eyes hanging out, for Pete's sake. Her bottom lip had been torn and, attached only by a slither of skin, had flopped over the bottom of her cheek, her lower teeth bared.

He'd have to visit their next of kin to inform them of the tragic news and, much as he detested it, ask them where they were this evening. That was standard, but it would be a loaded question because of the emotion involved in Codderidge's murder. Most killers, in his experience, didn't try to obliterate a face unless they were incensed with love or hate.

Or both.

"Got any thoughts for me, Evan?" Gary stood on an evidence step at the dead woman's feet, his white overalls rustling in a soft breeze. Jesus, it was so *cold* tonight.

Evan didn't turn his face to him. His bushy black eyebrows scrunched, and he swiped a gloved hand beneath blood-matted hair to brush it away from the victim's neck, some of it clinging to the bloodied gashes there. The photographer had already been, and Gary had given the all-clear for the pathologist to do his job, allowing him to touch the body if he had a mind. It'd be in his hands in the lab anyroad.

Evan sighed, his mask puffing out. "I'm thinking... And this isn't to tell you how to suck eggs with regards to working out what happened here."

"I always value your input. We're a team, all of us in it together." He was slightly sickened by saying that. He wasn't a full team member anymore, he was bent, but Trish... He was doing this for her, had to keep reminding himself of that. "You help with listening to the dead telling

344

their final story, and it always gives me something to run with. Go on."

"Kind of you to say. Gorley would have rolled his eyes—oh, and I have some news for you there, some findings from the post, although I haven't completed it yet. I'll tell you in a minute."

God…

Evan shifted on his haunches, his calf muscles probably giving him gyp. "Back to this case. Knight may have been hit to subdue him, get him out of the way while Codderidge was attacked. Perhaps the real rage was against *her*, not him, considering she's in this mess and he fared a little better, although that smack to his face, blunt force trauma with what I suspect was a bat—seen enough of those wounds to be certain that's what it is—was a pretty hard one, and the wounds on his neck, they'd have finished him off if the head blow didn't."

"So, a male assailant?"

Evan laughed, the hoot of an owl, his crows' feet concertinaing. "Come on now. You know as well as I do a woman could have done this. A bat, wielded by anyone angry enough, can create this kind of damage. As you've probably seen, it caved his forehead in, a bit of brain on show, skull fragments, whatever."

Gary winced. Evan's blasé way of describing things always unnerved him, but the man had seen all sorts of horrors at scenes and on his post-mortem table. He was probably desensitised, had to be to remain sane. Gary was sort of the same, although he had become jaded from seeing so much destruction so wasn't as jolly as the pathologist.

"But back to Codderidge," Evan said. "It appears several sharp implements at once entered not only her face but the top of her head—those in the skull are in a uniform pattern."

Gary's stomach muscles tightened. *Fuck it*. "Like barbed wire?"

"No, that would make an altogether different mess—and I said *uniform*, don't forget. Think of a scrubbing brush, except instead of bristles, you have pointed…nails maybe, or something of that nature. They're long."

A homemade weapon? Like Cassie's whip?

Gary always read *The Life* but had never done owt about what was written in the flyers, because there seemed to be hidden messages between the lines that only the civvy residents of the Barrington knew how to interpret. Of course, there was outright admittance of things, like the barbed wire whip, but unless Cassie was caught with it in her possession, the carrying of a weapon with intent to harm, or they suspected someone had been barbed by her, he couldn't very well walk up to her and demand to see it. No one who'd been barbed had come forward, and he reckoned they couldn't—they were most likely bloody dead. Over the years, officers at the station had either expressed their feelings or shown it on their faces when it came to dealing with things on the Barrington—no thanks, I'll stay away from there, let Lenny or Cassie deal with it.

Lenny had carved it in stone, the way things went, and while it was wrong for coppers to have let him—and now Cassie—go on their merry way, the Graftons were so canny, Gary doubted they'd be able to pin owt on them anyroad.

A waste of time and the public's money to drag them in for an interview.

He'd have to speak to Francis in a bit, about the possibility Cassie had made a second weapon.

Shit.

Evan glanced his way then back to the victim. "She's still warmish."

Gary's tummy churned. "That marries with what the man said about the time he found them."

One Dennis Abraham, a skinny young bloke, had come outside for a 'cheeky' cigarette 'innit' after the murders, texting his girlfriend while smoking and pacing, and he'd ventured as far as the wheelie bins, tripping on Codderidge's outstretched leg. He'd stumbled and righted himself by the time he'd met with a dead Knight—"It was nowt but a lump, like, cos it was dark."—and used his phone torch see what was ahead of him, then flashed it at Codderidge. One vomit session later, quite the splashback from several lagers and a plate of cheesy chips, his cigarette thrown in panic, Dennis had run to the back door, digested what he'd seen, and phoned the police.

No one else had witnessed a thing.

Good.

"So, about Gorley?" Gary held his breath. *Fuck knows what Evan has to say. Please let it just be a fire.*

"I'm afraid the weapon used on these two was probably also used on Gorley—not the bat, you understand, the other one."

Gary's body turned frozen, so, so cold. "How can you tell? From what I saw, all his skin was charred."

"Damage to the lower jaw bone and piercings in the gum and the flesh, the bones in his neck, striations caused by something like what I described, the nail scrubbing brush. He had three teeth missing, swallowing two, and they had to have been during an attack as the gums showed evidence of recent tooth removal."

He wasn't burnt enough, God, *he wasn't fucking burnt enough.*

"Okay, so were the teeth removed by another implement, say pliers during torture, or because of the weapon?"

"Once I get the chance to have another look, I'll be saying it's the weapon in my report. As you can imagine, the police deaths here, plus Gorley dead using the same tool, for want of a better word, and Bob missing… Four officers. Someone's out there picking you all off?"

I don't need this. "I bloody hope not."

"Me, too. I quite like you, and tending to your dead body isn't something I want to be doing." Evan rose and faced Gary. "Keep as safe as you can, pal. There are many nutters out there."

Don't I know it, and two are called Francis and Cassie. "I'll do my best."

Gary swivelled to find his DS, Kath Lowry, who stood by the pub door, bending to examine the handle for some reason. *Bloody hell, what now?*

"I'll catch you later, Ev." He left the evidence step, the crunch of grit beneath his shoes a crackle in the quiet.

"Yep, I'll be here for a while. Oh, and neither victim fought back, going by their fingernails, but that opinion may change once I scrape them. The attack was probably too quick for them to think of scratching the assailant."

"Cheers." Gary walked to Kath, imagining the fear his dead colleagues had experienced, hating himself for being prepared to cover owt up.

Another officer had joined Kath, one of the forensic lot, difficult to tell who as Gary didn't recognise their eyes above the mask.

"What's going on here then?" he asked. All he needed was to have added 'Hello, hello, hello' at the start to become a complete cliché, what with his home troubles, his need for a few scotches after work, and his defection of duty. He was a walking thriller novel detective, riddled with demons.

"I think something was used to force the handle up so it didn't come down." Kath pointed to the concrete just outside the door. "Wedged there. Look at the scrape on the ground."

There was no denying it, someone had done this to prevent smokers coming outside and spotting them in the act. *Bollocks*. Whoever they were had a set of balls on them. As a smoker himself, in their position, Gary would have gone out the front and come round here to have a puff—a blocked door wouldn't have stopped him.

"Okay, stick an evidence marker there. I just need to make a phone call to check on Trish, then I'll be back."

He strode down the side of the pub, signed the log, removed his booties (handing them over to the PC to put back on when he returned), then dipped beneath the cordon. He went left to stand beneath a lamppost, creating enough distance between him and the PC so he wasn't overheard. Undoing his protective clothing zip, he took the work burner Francis had given him out of his inside suit jacket pocket, casually glancing at the PC to ensure he wasn't being watched.

He wasn't.

While it was a risk to have the burner on him during shift hours, it was a necessity, one of her rules. He connected the call, and Francis answered quickly.

"Yes?"

"Possible problem," he said. "I'm at The Lion's Head."

"Oh dear. Can you handle it?"

So it *was* something to do with her. "Yes."

"Make sure you do. I hear Trish can't move out of her chair for the most part these days. It would be *such* a shame if someone broke in. She wouldn't be able to get away…"

Gary closed his eyes. "I hear you."

"Good man."

That was debateable. Good wasn't something he felt at the minute. "I'll need more money to deal with this."

"Of course you do. Tomorrow. A brown envelope in a Sainsbury's carrier bag in the bin outside Sam's Café. Ten a.m."

She cut him off, and he tucked the phone away, his whole body shaking.

What the *fucking hell* had he got himself into?

Chapter Eighteen

*F*our torturous weeks after Stalker's murder, Doreen meandered around the market. It was Saturday, her day off from the betting shop, and she couldn't stand to be in the house any longer. Stifling, that's what it was, and not only from the raging August heat. Mam had been on her earhole this morning about when she was going to move out again. Doreen couldn't wait to leave either, and she hadn't even been back long. God, if she could just find a room somewhere, she'd be gone like a shot.

She'd only lived with Lou and Janice for a few months, but in that time she'd grown used to doing her own thing without any questions, funny looks, or tsks. Mam had a nasty habit of poking her nose in whether Doreen wanted her to or not, and while she'd left home for just that reason, needing space and freedom, she hadn't realised how bad Mam was with her probing until she'd gone back. It seemed to have got worse, or maybe it just felt that way. Dad, bless his heart, sat in his chair, mouth shut, knowing from years of experience it was either do that or get his head chewed off.

Doreen never had been of a mind to copy him, take the lead he so obviously showed her, instead biting back at Mam if she was riled enough, baiting her in return, *and it always ended up with them shouting at each other, mother and daughter fighting for dominance, the matriarch usually winning.*

Doreen worried, with the murder and everything, whether her anxiety and fears meant she'd eventually cow down, be so browbeaten by her memories and thoughts that Mam's attacks would only serve to dim her light even more. So Doreen had made an attempt to stand up for herself. You know, remain the woman she'd been before she'd driven a blade into a man's stomach and across his throat, not some changed soul beneath a shell that masqueraded as who she used to be.

It was getting more difficult to put on a front, not easier.

"Oh, give over, Mam," Doreen had said, too loudly, too strident, her nerves so coiled she had the urge to punch the wall, something, anything to show Mam enough was enough. "I've been looking for a bedsit,

don't you worry. I mean, do you think I want to live here?"

"The cheek of it! My house was good enough to come back to, though, wasn't it. Oh yes, you were fine about coming here when it suited you."

"I didn't mean it like that, and you know it." God, why did Mam always have to put that spin on everything?

"Hmm. You never did say why you moved out of that lovely little place you had. Your own room, sharing the kitchen and bathroom with friends. It wasn't strangers you had to clean up after, was it, but people you already knew, and that makes a big difference. You won't get so lucky again, I'll be bound." Mam had folded her arms in that way she had, where it signalled a storm brewing; she was gearing up for a right old barny.

"I couldn't afford it in the end, even with the extra cash you gave me." Lie. "The gas meter scoffed so much money."

"Why? It's summer, you daft apeth. You don't use so much gas then. You need to learn to budget better, my girl, that's what I think. Gas, my eye. You've been spending too much time and money up The Donny and no mistake." Mam had nodded to herself: I'm right, you know I am, and my friends told me anyroad, so up yours, Dor. "And Lou hasn't been round since. Are you sure you haven't had a falling out?"

"She's busy, I'm busy, and we don't have the time to catch up now. She's taken extra shifts at Betty's, then there's that flower arranging course she's doing."

"Well, I'm sure I wouldn't know owt about that, because you never said until now. You don't share owt. Funny she hasn't nipped in, because you were in each other's pockets at one point. Something's happened, I know it; you just don't want to admit it."

Doreen had held back a scream. Mam was poking too hard at an abscess that might pop. "I'm not talking to you when you're in this kind of mood, it only leads to a row. I'm off to the market. Do you want owt?"

"A cauli and some carrots for tomorrow's roast."

Mam hadn't dipped her hand in her purse or said thank you.

Now, Doreen sighed and eyed a dress, but if she bought it, Mam would comment on it, saying how it was too short, too tight, and people would think Doreen was a tart if she 'swanned' up to The Donny in it. "Legs aren't for flashing, our Doreen."

She turned away from it, missing the nights she'd put on whatever she liked and Mam hadn't seen it, walking to the pub with Lou and Janice, having a right laugh, no chance of Mam turning up because she didn't hold with 'drinking and cavorting', unlike some people.

Christ, always there with a barb.

Bloody hell, maybe Doreen should have stayed with her friends, but it was too late now as some girl called Deborah had taken Doreen's place, and she doubted any of them would want her bunking in one of their rooms on a camp bed. And besides, Stalker calling her from the well had seemed so real at the time, and knowing his body was down the bottom of it... She couldn't cope with it. She swore a faint rotting meat smell had wafted out, too, the peat not doing enough to hide it, the summer so hot it drew the whiff up.

Lou had said, "But surely it'll be cold down there, so far under the ground, so the smell stayed there? You must have imagined it."

But I bloody didn't.

She moved on to the shoe stall, one with racks around the edges beneath the red-and-white-striped marquee. The woman who ran it wasn't about, probably gassing to someone elsewhere, another market trader, so Doreen browsed what was on offer, again telling herself not to bother buying any because…Mam. The old gal meant well, had a good heart when the chips were really down, but sodding hell.

"Those ones are nice," someone said in a Yorkshire accent.

Doreen turned to whoever had spoken, and her breath caught, her heart stalling. Eyes, those bloody blue eyes stared, and for one terrible second she thought they belonged to Stalker, that he'd clawed his way out of the well, taken himself to hospital, and was now all better. He couldn't have, though. It was too deep, there was no ladder, and it was just her silly mind playing tricks. And this man was a couple of inches taller, although he had the same colour hair, but it wasn't him, oh God, it wasn't him.

"Um, yes, they are nice but out of my price range," she barked, the need to run immense, gripping her

tight and begging her to get away from him, to take herself to safety, far from those eyes.

He smiled, coming off as an all right sort, and she felt bad for snapping.

"I wonder if you can help me. This might sound a bit weird, but I've been looking for someone, asking around, and the woman on the veg stall said to ask you. I arrived this morning, so just getting a feel for the place. It's confusing trying to find someone in a new town."

"Who are you after?" Fear clutched at her heart, even though he seemed kind and was as polite as owt.

"Lou—that's all I've got, I'm afraid, no surname. Do you know her?"

"What if I do? What business is it of yours?" Fucking hell, why was he looking for her? And why hadn't she asked: Lou who?

"It's just that she's my brother's girlfriend, and I need to find her. He hasn't phoned home for around a

month, nor has he written us any letters, and we're worried. Mam's going frantic, because his landlady hasn't heard from him either and wants her rent— Vera at the B&B. Mam thinks we might have to phone the police, report him as a missing person."

Doreen felt so sick she swallowed bile and had to steady herself with a hand on a pair of black patent high heels. "Lou doesn't have a boyfriend."

"So you do know her."

Doreen sniffed. "Listen, it must be the wrong Lou. Loads of people are called that. It's short for Louise, so yeah, lots of those about." She needed him to go away. This was getting a bit much. How could you feel cornered when you weren't in a corner? But she did, blocked in by his presence, his blue irises.

He smiled again. "The veg lady said I'd got it right. Lou works at Betty's Blooms, Steve said so."

"Steve?" 'S'. It had to be Stalker he was on about.

"My brother. I'm off there next as it happens, now I've been given directions. Steve wrote and said where she worked, that he'd met her in there."

I bet he didn't tell you what he did, how creepy he was, and that he followed her home so he'd know where she lived cos he'd planned to break into our house.

Her body went rigid, and she clutched his forearm, desperate to put an end to this. "I'll come with you. Let…let me speak to Lou first, before she sees you. She isn't into men, you see, not at the moment, so you saying she has a fella will throw her. Or maybe she is *seeing him and wanted to keep it a secret. I'll get it out of her, because she won't reveal owt like that to a stranger."*

"Okay."

In a bizarre turn of fate, Doreen led the way through the crowded market, the string bag with Mam's cauli and carrots banging her calf. People didn't bother shifting out of her way, so she had to elbow-barge them to part, and then there were the dirty looks, the "Oi, watch where you're bleedin' going!" The man kept pace beside her, and she at last found space, going down a ginnel that led to town. Betty's was two buildings along, so she stopped him outside the sweet shop.

"Stay here. I'll come and get you." Doreen walked off, checking over her shoulder that he wasn't following and, thankful he'd remained in place (browsing the jars of sweets in the window, a finger resting beneath his nose), she entered Betty's, nervous as anything, her chest tight with apprehension.

The woman herself stared at Doreen from behind the counter, the insolent cow, beady eyes assessing and finding Doreen wanting. "Look what the cat dragged in."

Doreen didn't like being referred to as a dead mouse but held back giving her the usual nasty retort. She

368

needed Betty on her side so had to be nice. "Sorry about this, but is Lou in?"

"Yes." Betty picked a leaf off a rose stem, one of many she was clipping. She tossed it on a blue tray beside the flowers.

"Can I see her?" Doreen fidgeted, waiting for a negative answer.

Betty scowled. "I don't pay her to gossip to the likes of you during working hours, you know. You don't earn money for talking—I assume that's what you two will be doing, chatting when she's meant to be making something for a customer."

"Please, it's important. I wouldn't normally ask, you know that, but I really need to see her."

Betty sighed. "She's out the back doing a bouquet for Mrs Watson. Her husband, Sid, asked us to make one as a surprise. Go through—but be quick about it. No dilly-dallying."

"Thanks." Doreen pushed through the doorway to the side of the counter, stepped into the flower arranging area, and shut them in.

Lou glanced up, a big smile transforming her somewhat pinched face—the murder had given her a haunted look, her skin sallow, faint shadows beneath her eyes.

Do I look like that?

"Ay up, Dor. It's great to see you, but we promised—"

Doreen flapped her hand, needing to stop Lou from blathering on, because she would, given half the chance. "I know, but fucking hell, something bad has gone on. Like, really bad."

Lou widened her eyes. "Oh God, is it your mam or dad? Has owt happened to them?"

"No. It's to do with Stalker."

Lou whimpered. She glanced at the door and pointed to it with a pair of small shears. "Whisper in

370

case Betty's got her ear pressed on that, you know how nosy she is. Shit, Dor, what's going on?"

"Stalker's brother came up to me at the sodding shoe stall, didn't he, saying he's looking for you. He knew your name."

Lou went white, and she blinked. A lot. "Why…why would he ask you?"

Doreen poked at the air in the direction of the flowers. "Because the stupid bitch you're making that bouquet for told him to."

"Mrs Watson?"

Was Lou being deliberately thick, or was Doreen cruel by thinking that?

"Yeah, he asked her on the veg stall. It doesn't matter how it went down, just that it did. He said he's looking for his brother's girlfriend, and that's you."

"But I'm not his bloody girlfriend. Why would he think that?"

Doreen stamped her foot. "I know, but he says you're it, Stalker told him you were—and he's called Steve, by the way."

"Who, the brother or Stalker?"

Doreen whimpered herself, frustration mounting. "Stalker!"

"How do you know he's owt to do with him, though?"

"He's got them weird eyes, hasn't he, just like him, and he said he hasn't heard from his brother for about a month."

"Oh shit. That ties in with…"

"Now you get it. I left him at the sweet shop."

"What?" Lou shrieked and dropped the shears. They clattered off the bench and onto the floor. She ignored them. "He's outside? Why?"

"Because he was coming here anyroad, and I thought it best I warn you. If he'd come on his own, you'd have shit yourself."

Lou turned away and fiddled with a white carnation petal, her bottom lip wobbling. "What are we going to say?"

"There's two options. One, you don't know who he's talking about, but then if he comes back here when you're not around, Betty's going to stick her ruddy great oar in, or you can say he was your fella but you haven't seen him for ages either. The problem with that is, he said his mam's on about phoning the police, so if they come to speak to you because you've admitted he was your boyfriend, they might find him down the well."

"Stop it, Dor. You're panicking. They won't find him down the well. They'd have to suspect he's there for a start, and why would they? No, the first option. I'm telling the truth, that he came in here being a weirdo, then just didn't come in anymore. Betty will back that up."

"Right. Come on then."

"Betty's not going to let me leave, I'm not due a break or lunch for ages, and I don't think I can face him. You tell him. Get him to talk to Betty if you have to, but stay with him so you know what's said."

Doreen walked out, disregarded Betty, and rushed outside. The man had moved along and now stood next door at the butcher's, although he didn't study the meat but looked across the high street. She reached his side, and he turned to her and gave her that lovely smile. If he wasn't owt to do with a murdered man, she might have considered asking him out.

"I've had a natter with Lou. She's not his girlfriend, but he did come in a few times about a month back, buying flowers then giving them to her, writing strange poems on the cards—which is a bit odd, don't you think? He asked her out for a drink, but she said no; he came back about five times after that, then she didn't see him again. Lou's busy at the minute, but come and see Betty, she'll tell you." She grabbed his arm and tugged him into the florist shop.

"Not you again," Betty said, then copped the man. "Oh, you look like that fella who was after Lou."

A conversation ensued, him explaining why he was there, Betty telling him all about the flower-buying shenanigans.

"But he's not Lou's boyfriend," Betty said. "I know her mam really well, and she hasn't said owt, and neither has Lou." She addressed Doreen. "Is he her bloke?"

"No! Lou hasn't seen him since the last time he bought flowers."

Betty tucked some straggly grey hair behind her thick-lobed ear, a gold daisy earring clipped so tight the flesh bulged around it. "Neither have I, come to think of it." She eyed the man. "Sorry, duck, we can't help you. Gone missing, you said?"

"Hmm."

Betty slammed a palm on the counter. "Then it's a police matter. I'm happy to speak to them, tell them he came in here, but as for knowing where he is, I don't have a clue."

He nodded his appreciation. "Thank you for your time. I'll visit his landlady next. Vera."

Doreen's stomach hurt. "Good luck."

He walked out, and she sighed with relief.

"Nice man, that Steve—that's what he said his name was, wasn't it?" Betty asked.

"Yes. Can I just nip back in to Lou, tell her what was said?"

Betty gave a rare smile. "Only if you make me a brew while you're out there. A splash of milk, three sugars."

Doreen darted into the back room, closing the door. "He's gone. Betty saved us."

Lou rubbed her watery eyes. She must have been crying. "God, this is so awful."

"I know." Doreen patted her friend's arm. "But…secret forever."

Chapter Nineteen

God, Jason was so *irritating*. Just seeing him tested Cassie's patience. There had been times since becoming Dad's right hand where she only had to look at certain people and she wanted to punch them in the face, for no reason other than they had a way about them that set her off.

She'd often wondered whether her angst at having to run the patch instead of becoming a teacher surged to the fore during those times. Did she want to take her rage out on them, on anyone, so she felt better?

Someone would suggest a therapist next. "Get your head tested, Cassie, you're off your sodding rocker."

Maybe she was.

Or was she, despite thinking otherwise before joining the family business, born bad? Born to hurt and maim and kill? The nature versus nurture subject had taken up a lot of headspace at first. After all, she'd thought she was a 'normal' person, someone who didn't like violence (especially when Dad had told her exactly what he did), but perhaps his teachings had encouraged that part of her out from where it had been slumbering deep inside her.

Or he'd fashioned her monster all by himself, moulding her mindset like some creepy cult leader, changing her views, her ideals, keeping on and on until she accepted herself for who he'd created. Except she hadn't accepted it, not fully. Instead, she'd compartmentalised. There was good Cassie, then there was the monster.

How could he do that to her, his *child*?

More and more, she was coming to the conclusion he wasn't as idol-like as she'd thought. A man who could direct their wife to do what she did, what Jason did, what all the residents did, then got Cassie to do the same… *He* wasn't right in the head. And as for Mam, well…

Cassie shut those thoughts off; too painful, too revealing. She glared down at Jason. He didn't return it, his gaze on the bookshelf, making it so obvious he either wanted her to know she wasn't important enough for him to look at or he plain didn't want to. Stubborn dickhead. Maybe he thought she was beneath him, someone not worthy of his attention, taking a leaf out of his mother's book by snubbing her. Or perhaps he couldn't stop staring at what was on *top* of that shelf and he was shitting bricks.

But he'd maintain eye contact eventually, she'd make sure of it, even if only for a brief second—that would be victory enough. His breathing indicated his agitated state, although his body language portrayed nowt. Here was a man who'd taken Lenny's teachings to heart: *Never let your opponent know what you're thinking.*

She smiled. He'd wish he'd never taken Lenny's offer of working for him by the time she'd finished with him, or perhaps he already did—was regret suffocating him? No, knowing Jason, he thought this was a torture warning and she'd get Dr Flemming to sort his leg and face in some underground operating theatre—like that was even a thing. Flemming was good, but not that good.

And Cassie was lenient sometimes, but not that lenient.

Her work phone bleeped, and she checked WhatsApp.

Mam: *Two bacon rashers found. Being dealt with.*

It was inevitable but sooner than Cassie had hoped. She'd thought the darkness in the yard at The Lion's Head would have prevented anyone from seeing the bodies should they go out there to smoke. Tomorrow morning would have been better for the discovery of the pigs, but so long as Gary Branding was in charge, things would be smoothed over. If they weren't and the police paid them a visit, none of the neighbours would admit Cassie, Mam, and Lou had gone out at a certain time, returning later. Then there was

Nicola from The Pudding. Cassie had told her they were having a night in, and she'd force her to say just that if necessary. And if Branding didn't shush this up, he'd be meeting Marlene. Alive. Cassie and Mam would watch the mincer scoffing him up, listen to his screams…

Cassie: *Okay*.

She slid her phone in her pocket and eyed Jimmy, who stood by the window, the top half of his shadow large and misshapen on the blind. The bottom appeared elongated, the thighs stretching down the old-fashioned yellowing radiator with its tumbleweeds of dust on top, shin shapes on the floor, the feet joining his, as if the shadow were his soul and couldn't bear to break contact.

"He's ever so rude, don't you think?" she asked him.

Jimmy started, clearly uncomfortable with being brought into this, to have to give an opinion. "Yeah, well rude." He gave an awkward smile that said: *Sorry, I'm not used to this shit, but I'm trying.*

She shifted her attention to Jason again, studying his gross bottom lip, and the urge to squeeze it between finger and thumb overcame her. *Christ, what's the matter with me?* She wanted to hurt and hurt and hurt him, no holds barred. What *was* it, driving her to do it? An in-born need, a Lenny-manufactured one, the proof Jason wanted the estate?

Or was it his betrayal?

Once again, she shut her thoughts down. "Where were you going to get the anti-depressants from to drug me and my mam? Which seller were you going to approach? Or have you already done that? If it's someone working for me, I want to know about it. But then again, you're not thick, so I bet you were going to the Sheffield lot, or maybe the pushers in Doncaster."

Jason continued ogling the bookshelf as if she hadn't spoken, no tells to indicate which option was the correct one. He must want her to think someone else in her pay was a mole, prepared to go against her. He'd know damn well that would drive her up the wall trying to work it out.

Was he imagining the pain he'd go through when she used what was on top on the bookshelf? How many times she'd inflict it? How long before she administered the fatal move and all this ended? Did he *want* it to end? Was he in that much pain he wished he was dead, even if that meant leaving his mother?

"I'd have gathered what you were doing to us anyroad," she said. "We'd have noticed how we felt, groggy or whatever. Especially because you told Jimmy you planned to put it in my coffee and food when we went out on dates, get me dependent, then chat enough shit to convince me to let you move in, then you'd start on Mam. My *mam*, Jason. That's so wrong. How would you feel if I planned to do that to yours?"

His lips twitched.

"You really are a minger. Disloyal. Still, *Jimmy* was loyal, which brings us to this point. Did you *really* think you'd get away with it, that he wouldn't tell me?"

He ignored her.

"I bet Gina will be on my earhole soon, asking if I've seen you—note she hasn't bothered to yet. That must sting, your mammy not caring enough to find out where you are." She smiled, the perfect piss-him-off words forming in her head. "I'm undecided on what to do there. You know, tell her you went missing in the proper sense, just walked off after we'd had a falling out... Or that I barbed your face up then shot you in the leg with a fucking nail, and *then*, I killed you, minced your body, and scattered bits of it all over the Barrington. I might even go as far as to mention the foxes that may have eaten you, the birds pecking at the meat. Can you *imagine* the horror and pain she'll feel when she hears that?"

He growled, just like those foxes. "Uck you."

"It's *fuck*, Jason."

"Izz ov."

"No. There's still so much to discuss. Let's see..." She rested a finger on her cheek, drawing things out and loving it. The monster had arrived. "Nathan Abbott. A man down on his luck, then Lenny came along and offered him a job looking after that set of sex workers, got him back on his feet. Is that why you chose Nathan? I mean, you must have thought *you* were the only man Lenny felt something for, yet here comes Nathan, being looked after by him, too. I can't believe you'd do this to my dad. Lenny *cared* for you."

"Ee dint."

"He didn't? What do you call it when someone takes you under their wing then? How could he *not* care if he killed your fucking *dad*? If he saved you and your mam from him?"

Jimmy let out a grunt of surprise, and Cassie glanced his way.

"This is what happens, Jim. Graftons do what needs to be done for residents. Jason here, his father liked to call him names all the time, hurt Gina, give her black eyes and shit, rule the house like a proper rotten bastard. Lenny stopped all that, and what does Jason do? He tells himself he'll take the crown, that's what, throwing everything Lenny did for him back in his face.

Well…" She stared at Jason. "You forgot one thing. I'm Lenny's daughter, and I will *not* allow you to ride roughshod over me—or his memory. Come on, admit it. You didn't think I had it in me, did you? You thought I'd be crap at running the patch. What do you think *now*?"

Jason shuddered and cried out from the movement. A groan followed, and she'd bet he wanted to close his eyes. Too bad he couldn't. How dry must his eyeballs be if he couldn't blink?

She raised her leg as though about to kick him.

"No! Peas, no."

She lowered her foot to the floor. At least she knew he was afraid of what she'd do. His usual bravado was waning; he couldn't keep it up forever.

"Back to Nathan—because I have a huge problem with killing him. I did it based on your information—and it was *wrong*. How does it feel to lay the blame at another man's door when it was yours? *You* skimmed those takings, not him. *You* let me torture him, kill him, mince him, while knowing he hadn't done a thing. I believed you so much that when he told us he hadn't done owt, I didn't listen to him, so you can congratulate yourself on that, how clever you were, how convincing. What you probably won't realise now, though, is you did me a favour. I'll *never* trust my right hand again, even if I choose Mam, Doreen, or Glen Maddock."

His eyeballs moved momentarily at that—Glen Maddock. He'd hate that fella taking his place. He'd been Dad's right hand, and bloody good at it he was, too.

"He's a decent fella, never let Lenny down. But you did. By being such a nasty bastard in all this, you let down the one man who took you on as a son. Your own father didn't give a fuck, but mine did." She paused, getting ready to say the one word Jason hated when it was aimed at him. "Yours just called you a prick."

Another skin-stiff flinch.

"And that's exactly what you are. A lying, deceitful, waste-of-space *prick*."

He roared an intelligible stream of shite and looked at her, eyes bulging, and if she wasn't mistaken, his face wounds cracked in places. Yes, they had. Fresh blood trickled, meandering down the hardened flesh, red rivers over crusty rocks.

"Mind you don't hurt yourself." She laughed until her sides hurt—to release the tension in her coiled muscles or because she was enjoying this?

"No thinking. Just get the job done, Cass."

Her spine straightened at Lenny's words, and she went to the bookshelf.

Jason snorted air through his nostrils. "No…"

"Yes."

She opened the case and took out what she needed. Turned to him. Held it to her chest. "You know what this means, don't you, Jason."

"Fuck," Jimmy whispered.

Jason's fingers played piano. "Peas."

"Stop going on about fucking *peas*, pal." Cassie moved to the electric socket. Slid the plug in. "The choice is yours for the first shot. Your other leg or your arm?" She held the nail gun up and waved it about. "Eight lovely inches. Who'd have thought they'd cause so much *pain*." She stepped closer. "Jimmy, free his wrists from behind him."

Jimmy obeyed and placed Jason's arms across his stomach. One flopped to the floor. Jimmy returned to the window.

Cassie smirked. "Just think, if I shoot that arm there, the one over your belly, the nail will go into your guts an' all."

Perhaps the instinct to get away overrode Jason's need to stay put. He tried to get up, and his pinned shin lifted, the nail disappearing beneath the bone. His elongated scream got on Cassie's tits, and anger at him still not conceding defeat burnt through her.

"Admit to me you were going to take the patch," she shouted. "Tell me to my face you wanted to ruin me. Have you got the balls?"

She aimed the gun and shot his upper arm, securing it to his side.

Pain. So much pain. It fired through Jason's whole body, the tip of the nail digging into whatever innards were beneath the pierced skin. As for the one in his shin...his leg had gone numb. Maybe him jolting like that had done something to the nerves.

Faint from the pain, he fought the need to tell her what she wanted to know, the insistent bitch. Part of him reckoned she'd set him free if he did—surely she wouldn't kill Lenny's surrogate son? And they'd got along fine until he'd blabbed about his mission. Well, as fine as you *could* get along with Cassie. Didn't she have any feelings for him? He'd been in her life for a long time.

Don't you have any feelings for her other than to bring her down?

No.

So why should she feel anything for you?

A bigger part of him whispered that she'd murder him for this.

How odd to know that inside a few minutes, his life would end.

What she'd said about Mam. Fuck, why hadn't his mother rung Cassie yet? He knew the answer to that; it was stupid to ask himself that question: he'd told her he'd be away some nights for work and not to worry about him if he didn't come home.

Why had he opened up to Jimmy in The Donny, trusted him?

Because he hadn't thought he was in Cassie's pay yet.

The voice murmured, *"But she mentioned something about bringing him into the business. Didn't you listen?"*

Obviously not. Or he'd ignored it, thinking she was talking bullshit.

That was his problem, he could see that now: he always knew best. But he fucking well didn't, and Cassie was giving it her all in letting him know that.

"You're a waster, Jason. A fucking prick, son."

He growled at his father's voice.

His arm was more than on fire now, and he teetered on the ledge, ready to sink into oblivion again. At least then he wouldn't see her coming at him with that bloody nail gun. He wouldn't know he was dead if he was out of it.

He pushed past the agony, telling himself to admit what he'd done. See if she'd let him go if he did. He had to try, didn't he? But only if the pain got too much. He'd confess it then.

In the meantime, he needed to remain awake— his ego wouldn't let him do otherwise at the minute—if only to prove to her how strong he still was, how she didn't call the shots.

Even though she had that gun to administer them in a different way.

And he had no doubt she would.

What's going through his head? Is he even thinking of owt other than the pain?

Jason calmed, slumping back down, blood welling then oozing out of the shin wound, spreading over his creepy shaved leg. More blood coated his sleeve and the area where the nail had entered his side. He breathed heavily, and his eyes rolled. Cassie reckoned he was on the verge of passing out so needed to do this quickly.

"Admit it."

He remained silent. Why was he being so stubborn? Was it that much of a trial to just say what he'd done?

She poked at his injured arm, and he squealed, panted.

"I'm not going to stop until I hear what I want," she said. "You know enough about me by now to realise that. I'm a dog with a bone, gnawing and gnawing. And like a dog, I'll bury you—but not in the ground." She didn't say he'd be in pigs' bellies.

Time stretched.

Jimmy paced, a hand to his forehead. "How much longer are you going to drag this out, Jason? For fuck's sake, she isn't going to back down. Just tell her, will you?"

Jason sighed, and Cassie fancied it was one of resignation—he was beaten and he knew it.

He managed, "Oh-gay, I...wan tid it."

Victory soared through Cassie, and she couldn't stop the winner's smirk. "I know you did. But guess what?" She bent over him. "You're not going to have it." She nailed his hand to his belly, the round end pushing his skin and flesh inwards.

You absolute knob.

He had some kind of fit, jerking, his tongue poking out. Garbled sounds came from his ruined mouth, unfinished words and "Peas, peas…" She stepped over him, one foot on either side. Gun pointing at his heart, close, she shot him again, abandoning her earlier idea of shooting him in the eye, intent on killing him a faster way while he was still with it, so he'd feel the pain and know he'd soon take his final breath.

Blood. It spurted, landing on the ends of her dangling red hair, her clothes. He choked, scarlet filling his mouth and running out of the sides, dripping onto his top. His irises lowered then lifted out of sight, and his body relaxed. One last tremor in his good leg, his heel whacking the floor, and he was gone.

"Christ alive." Jimmy stopped pacing and slapped a hand over his mouth.

"This is what happens when you cross me, Jim. I get a bit angry, like."

He came to stand beside her. "You didn't *look* angry."

She straightened, reversing away from Jason, then tugging the plug out of the socket. "Good. That means Lenny taught me well." She coiled the cord around the handle of the gun and walked over to put it back in the case, returning to stand at Jason's feet.

Jimmy couldn't seem to stop staring at him. "What happens next?"

"We take him to see Marlene."

"But he's already dead. She can't kill him again, cos that's what she does, isn't it?"

Cassie chuckled. "Oh my days, you do make me laugh. You'll see soon enough. Now, are you going to help me yank him off that nail in the floor or do I have to do it myself?"

Chapter Twenty

Alone in his car on the drive to the meat factory (and he'd never felt so alone in his life), Jimmy couldn't get the sound of Jason's flesh ripping out of his head, a squelch and tear combined, repeating over and over.

When they'd each grabbed him beneath an armpit and hauled him off that nail… God, they'd had to tug for a bit, then the shin broke free, the nail coming away with it, leaving a hole in the carpet in the middle of a soaked-in circle of blood. Cassie, gloves on, had yanked the nail out of the calf and held the bloodied thing up to the light, turning it this way and that as though marvelling at how such a simple thing could rip into skin and bone the way it had.

Jimmy had trembled all over, still holding Jason's armpit, unable to believe for a second what he was doing—he was *there*, a dead man's back against his legs, his new boss smiling in such a creepy manner he'd had to look away.

Fucking hell. What have I got myself into here?

It was too late to ask himself that now. He was in it up to his neck.

While the lure of twenty grand was strong and could send him and Shirl on a lovely holiday and clear their debts, he asked himself whether the money was worth all the nightmares he was bound to have—there was no way he'd sleep soundly, was there. He'd never forget how Cassie had so casually unplugged that nail gun (and that act was somehow more frightening than the murder itself), as if she didn't have any feelings one way or the other about what she'd done to Jason—and God knew who else.

She'd mentioned Nathan Abbott (Jimmy had wondered where he'd got to), and that Jason had taken some money and blamed it on him. Yeah, that was a mega shitty thing to do, and Jason *did* deserve pain as punishment, but to the degree Cassie had administered it?

Jimmy wasn't so sure about that, but who was he to question the patch leader? He couldn't very well tell her he thought she'd gone way over the top and expect to live afterwards. From now on, he was stuck in her employ, and if he valued his life, he'd accept that and do whatever she asked, ignoring the voice inside him that said this was wrong, all of it. Yeah, he'd grown up knowing what living on the Barrington meant, but there was listening to rumours and seeing it for yourself, two completely different things.

And he couldn't *un*see it. Would he tell Shirl everything? He didn't know. She was a nice woman, kind, and it might upset her. But she worked for Cassie now, too, so was it better to warn her about this shit? Get her accustomed to what she might face? Was he even *allowed* to pass on the events of the night?

Jason intruded into his thoughts. Had he had time to feel that nail going into his heart, or had it been so fast he hadn't registered it? Had Cassie shut down her emotions in order to kill him, or had she liked it, allowing those emotions to rule her with an iron fist that matched the one she employed on the Barrington?

Jimmy couldn't decide. A mask had come down over her face when she was in what he could only assume was 'the zone', an impenetrable one where however much he'd scrutinised her features, he hadn't been able to make out what she felt while triggering that last nail.

Did he really want to know, though? Finding out what made her tick was a step in the 'I'm fucking mental if I do that' direction. Her revealing *feelings* and, dare he even think it, enjoyment might mean *he'd* get infected with whatever warped creature inhabited her at these times, be changed, the old Jimmy no more.

Face it, pal, the old Jimmy has died now anyroad.

She'd gone out to the car and come back with a body bag—where the hell could you buy *those*, for Pete's sake? Together, they'd placed him inside, and that zip going up, the rasp of it, had Jimmy shivering. It was such a final sound, so *he's dead*.

Cassie had phoned her crew to come and rip up the carpet, wash the flooring beneath, and the walls. Then she'd arranged for some fella to nip by tomorrow to lay lino—"Much better for when we need to mop up," she'd said. "I don't know why my dad didn't think of it, what with having to keep scrubbing that bloody manky carpet."

We? Was Jimmy supposed to help her with this shit on a regular basis? He was, he knew that now, he'd be a fool to tell himself otherwise, no matter that she'd said she wouldn't make him do it. How would he cope? Would he become as hardened as her? He was soft, maybe too soft in some eyes, but Shirl liked that about him. She'd said the other men she'd been out with before him didn't show how they felt.

"But you, Jimmy, you're different. Don't ever change on me, will you."

He was bound to, though, when dealing with blood and torture and murder and—

Pissing Nora. Concentrate on this and think later.

Ahead of him, Cassie turned onto the track that led to the factory, and he followed, shuddering at the fact she had a body in her boot—and that Marlene was waiting for them. How did the woman know they were coming? He hadn't seen Cassie messaging her, and she certainly hadn't phoned her. Or maybe she'd given her a bell on the way here, instructing her to meet them.

Crikey, he wasn't sure how to act around Marlene. What should he do, stick his hand out for her to shake it, like she wasn't some murdering cow? Say, "Pleased to meet you" while crapping his kecks, all the while *not* pleased to meet her in the bloody slightest? And why was she involved if Jason was already dead?

Maybe she's the one who buries all the bodies.

Then why did Cassie say we were going inside *the factory? Can't she just let Marlene take the body bag and be done with it?*

He stopped round the back of the factory beside Cassie's car. She was already out and at the door, which was propped open by her arse, the light on in a corridor. The faint bleep of the alarm snuck into his car, out of sync with his heartbeat. She poked at some buttons, and silence returned. Well, as silent as it could be with his pulse thudding inside his aching head and his breathing going skew-whiff.

He left his vehicle, stepping in the patches where the snow had melted, and walked towards Cassie, his legs wobbly. Delayed shock, he reckoned. She propped the door open with a black rubber stopper wedged beneath it, and he stood in front of her, wondering what the fuck was coming next.

"I'll just go and get the trolley." She turned to go down the corridor.

Jimmy frowned. What the chuff was going on? She'd said that as if he should know. "Trolley?"

She peered over her shoulder. "To take the body inside."

Off she went, leaving Jimmy once again querying why the hell Jason had to be taken indoors. This wasn't making sense.

At the sound of a vehicle rumbling, he jumped, nerves so frayed his neck hurt from tension. He inched along the building, shitting himself, arriving at the corner and peering round.

Headlights. Whoever it was came from the direction of the Barrington. He held his breath as they drove closer, then his guts rolled over because... *Fuck me, they're coming here.*

He legged it to the factory door and, about to enter, halted, bracing himself with a hand on the frame, his chest tightening. *I want to go home to Shirl.*

Cassie pushed a long steel trolley towards him, her mask in place again.

"Someone's coming," he panted out, ready to shove the trolley so she had to go backwards, then he could lock them in, get them safe.

But what about the body? What if they find it? What if it's the bloody police?

Cassie sighed. "Give over, it's only Ted and Felix. Move your arse, will you, I need to get past."

"Ted and Felix?" He was parroting her again, annoyed with himself for doing it, and stepped aside to let her out, so bewildered he wished he hadn't agreed to record Jason's confession. Wished he hadn't agreed to *any* of this. "What do *they* want?"

Cassie moved past him, the trolley wheels creating a right old noise on the concrete—thank God the factory was away from any houses and no one would hear it. At her boot, she opened it. "Help me dump this wanker on there."

Jimmy swallowed. Joined her. If his breathing could just go back to normal, that'd be grand.

A car rounded the corner, further spiking his adrenaline; it flooded his system and threatened to send him keeling over. The small runaround parked beside Jimmy's, the driver's door opening, the interior light splashing on. It was Ted and Felix all right, men people wouldn't have thought were involved in this side of the Grafton business.

Then again, look how tight they were with Lenny.

He should have known they'd be in on shit to this degree. Hindsight was so spiteful the way it taunted you for not seeing, not putting two and two together at the time, and it laughed at him for being such an oblivious fool.

The old men approached, Felix standing next to Jimmy, Ted by Cassie. All four of them stared into the boot, Jimmy hating what was beneath that material—not Jason, although he disliked him, but the body, the mess.

"Thank God you saw the bleedin' light with this one." Ted poked a finger towards the shrouded Jason, clearly visible from the glow in the boot. "I'm glad you rang. I'm more than happy to see what Marlene does to him."

Fucking hell, does she mutilate dead bodies or what?

"You never did like him, did you?" Felix said.

Ted shook his head. "He was a trumped-up twat like his mother." He nudged Cassie. "No offence, like, but why your old man thought it was a good idea for Jason to be your right hand is beyond me. Trying to take over the patch. What a dickhead."

"We've got Jimmy to thank for getting the confession." Cassie patted Jimmy's shoulder. "And he held up well at the squat."

"Champion." Ted smiled at him. "I like you, Jim, always have. How's Shirl?"

Was that some kind of threat? Jimmy wasn't sure how to take it so nodded. "She's all right, ta. You?"

"All the better for being here, lad." Ted rubbed his latex-gloved hands. "Come on then, let's get going."

Turned out Jimmy didn't need to help after all. Old they might be, but Ted and Felix lifted the body bag out and all but threw it onto the trolley. Jimmy winced at how that must hurt, then remembered Jason wouldn't feel a thing. The cousins manoeuvred the trolley into the factory, whistling in harmony, and Cassie closed the boot, the light dousing.

"This is usually their job, taking people to Marlene," she said. "And they dispose of the bodies afterwards. Anyroad, like Ted just said, come on, let's get going."

He followed her into the factory, hating being there, asking himself if he'd fallen asleep at the squat and was only dreaming, but the floor was too solid beneath his feet, the surroundings too real. Cassie closed the door and led the way to another one, which stood open. Inside a small room, Ted and Felix stood by a steel machine. Jimmy trailed Cassie inside and gazed around. A sink unit was off to the right, and some tall plastic boxes with lids stacked on top had been placed by a thingy (he couldn't think what it might be called, his brain blank) that stuck out of the machine. A steel hose? On top was a large chute with steps leading up to it.

Where was Marlene?

"Okay, let's have a gander at him." Ted pulled the zip down on the body bag and parted the fronts so the space created a white elm leaf shape. "Oh, fuck me, would you look at the state of him." He laughed, his cheeks going red, his grey fringe wafting.

Felix leant forward. "You used your weapon again, Cass."

She nodded. "Of course I did. He needed the pain."

There she is, all casual again.

"That must have been right sore." Felix grimaced and squinted. "What's up with his lip?"

Cassie shrugged. "I split it with a barb and sewed it back up."

Felix shook his head. "Blimey, girl, I worry about you."

"No need."

"Um, what else did you do to him?" Felix bent even closer and inspected the shin and sliced trousers. "That's a fair-sized hole, that is."

"Eight-inch nail. There's holes in his arm, hand, and heart an' all." Cassie folded her arms. Was that a defensive move or one that said: *And? I have to answer to you because?*

Ted laughed even more. "Good. He deserved the agony. Horrible little twat."

Felix wiped his brow. "You shot him. With a nail gun." He closed his eyes for a second. "Does Gina know?"

"Not yet." Cassie tapped her foot. "Are you trying to tell me something or just being fucking nosy?"

Felix held both hands up. "No, no, only asking, making conversation, like."

"Probably better if you don't." Cassie gave one of her weird tight smiles. "I'm not in the mood."

Ted and Felix stared at each other, raised their shoulders simultaneously, and got to work, taking Jason out then undressing him, Ted using a penknife to cut around the material near the nail heads in the arm, then slicing the rest away. He used pliers to wrench the nails out. All the while, Jimmy watched, everything so surreal. And Marlene *still* hadn't turned up. What was keeping her? If the old men dumped the bodies, why did the woman even need to be here?

A naked Jason wasn't a sight Jimmy ever thought he'd see, the traitor's clothes and the nails in a pile on the floor.

"Oh, he's hairless all over." Cassie shuddered.

"Even round his meat and two veg!" Ted roared with laughter.

"I bet he's even had his arsehole waxed," Felix said.

Jimmy couldn't get over how they acted so *normal*.

Cassie swept the clothes and nails up and stuffed them into a carrier bag she got out from under the sink, the supermarket logo on the side, something so familiar but alien at the same time. Ted gripped Jason's ankles, and Felix tucked his hands beneath the armpits. Felix walked backwards up the steps then moved to the side to feed Jason's head and shoulders into the chute.

"Go on, fire her up," he said.

Jason's going in there*?*

Cassie pressed a button, and the machine rumbled to life, something grinding inside. Ted went up two steps, pushing Jason farther until his arse sat on the lip of the chute. Together, they gave him a shove.

"That's it, Marlene girl, you eat him up," Ted shouted.

The *machine* was Marlene? *What?*

Jimmy turned to Cassie, who smiled.

"It never was a woman," she yelled over the din. "People just assumed."

Jimmy glanced back at the chute. It had flesh and blood on the inside, spatter from where the machine—*Marlene!*—went to work. The heels of Jason's feet rested on the lip now, and Marlene's sound changed—fuck, some kind of grinding was going on. Cutting up his head? Jimmy heaved, his hand over his mouth, and then movement to his left grabbed him, and he stared in horror at mince coming out of the thingy.

Oh my fucking God.

He ran to the sink and spewed, his mind spinning, his heart racing, coffee the first to emerge, then bile burning his throat.

Cassie's loud laughter floated over, and he knew then, without a shadow of a doubt, that sometimes, she really was mad.

Chapter Twenty-One

The Barrington Life

MISSING MAN ALERT!

Karen Scholes – All Things Crime in our Time
Sharon Barnett – Chief Editor

EDITION ONE

Me and Sharon reckon this is the easiest way to let you all know things at once regarding crime and such on the estate. Saves us spreading the gossip, and I've never been a fan of Chinese whispers. Whenever something really important goes on, we'll be posting these flyers from now on. Dunno why we didn't think of this before. Mind, the expense of getting them printed is a bit much, so we won't be doing it often — at least not until we can afford one of those fancy computers.

I was in Betty's Blooms the other day, and she told me some fella has gone missing. About a month ago, it was — well, more like five weeks now — a bloke from Yorkshire; young lad, dark hair, blue eyes, about twenty or so. He'd been living on the Barrington, renting a room at Vera's, like, so that makes it our business. He's called Steve, by the way, no idea what his surname is.

Anyroad, his brother came to look for him because the family hadn't heard owt for weeks, and he asked our Lou at Betty's Blooms if she was seeing him, because that's what this Steve had said. Well, Lou only knew him from when he'd gone into the florist's to buy flowers, and she certainly wasn't his girlfriend.

So, the point of this flyer is, if you've seen a man around with really blue eyes, and you made friends with him or whatever, if you know owt, contact the police. It doesn't sit well that someone's gone missing from our estate, so let's do the decent thing and band together to find Steve so his family can get answers.

Incensed at her name being in the flyer, Lou scrunched it up and threw it in the bin. Saturdays were meant to be for relaxing and catching up on her washing, not getting angry and wanting to strangle Karen and Sharon. Who they thought they were she didn't know. The way they gadded about on the estate as if they owned it got right on her nerves, but people appeared to be listening to the pair of silly cows, doing whatever they told them.

425

Well, Lou wasn't one of those people, especially when any poking about into Stalker's disappearance meant her and Doreen could be right up the swanny.

She called out to Janice and Deb that she was off out and left the house, storming up the road towards Doreen's mam's. Yes, they'd promised to keep apart, but this visit was needed, as was the one Doreen had made to Betty's. It was all very well saying they'd avoid each other—which was stupid anyroad because who'd suspect them of murder?—but when shit like this happened, they had to speak face to face.

In Doreen's road, she took a deep breath and marched up to the front door. Penny answered, Dor's mother, her smile bright, her arms held out in welcome. Odd. Lou smiled and reared back to avoid being grabbed for a hug.

Penny lowered her arms. "How are you, duck?"

"All right, ta. Is Dor in?"

"In her room, as usual."

Penny stepped back, and Lou entered, grabbed by Penny anyroad and squeezed too hard.

"We've missed you," she said. "Why did you stop coming round?" Then she whispered in her ear, "Did you two fall out?"

Lou extracted herself and moved to the safe distance of the stairs. "No, we haven't had a row or owt. I was a bit busy, that's all."

"Still, you're here now." Penny closed the door and made to approach.

Lou skittered up the stairs, unnerved by Penny's unusual display of emotion. She'd always been brusque before, and Lou suspected it was all a play so she could whisper what she had. Of course it would look weird that Lou no longer came here now Dor was back. She'd been here so often in the past her absence was bound to be noted.

On the landing, she breathed deep again and knocked on the bedroom door.

"I said I was having a nap," Dor shouted.

"It's me." Lou turned the handle and poked her head inside.

Dor scrabbled to sit up, flapping her hand for Lou to come in. She did and, door closed, sat on the bed.

"What the hell are you doing here?" Dor kept her voice low.

"Didn't you read the flyer the two bitches sent?"

Dor smiled. "Which two bitches? There are loads on this estate."

"Karen and Sharon."

Dor shook her head. "No. What are they sending flyers for?"

"Apparently, it's a new thing they're doing when anything criminal happens. Karen moaned about the printing costs, so hopefully we won't get another one for a while."

"Crime?" Dor paled and darted a glance at the door. "Whisper in case Mam comes nosing."

"It had Stalker in it."

"What?" Dor shrieked then slapped a hand over her mouth.

"You said to whisper, you silly cow."

"I know, but… What were they saying about him?"

"That he's missing and his brother came to find him, and if anyone knows owt, they should go to the police." Lou thought of what state the body would be in by now at the bottom of the well. "The smell's gone and—"

"So you did smell it."

Lou shrugged. "Only a bit."

"You made me think I'd imagined it."

Lou huffed. "I had to calm you down somehow, didn't I?" She sighed. "What if this doesn't go away? What if all the residents start poking about? The neighbours either side of me… What if they smelt him, too, and realise it was strange, then call the pigs? What if they come round and ask to look in the well? The water board's already been out for blocked drains, but they didn't find anything, obviously."

"You told me not to worry about that when I brought it up, so take your own advice. Have the police spoken to you yet?"

"Yes, at Betty's. We gave the same story, and they seemed okay with that. Bob Holworth, it was, and you know he fancies me, so it won't go anywhere, I bet."

"It had better not." Dor bit her lip. "I have nightmares every so often. Do you?"

Lou nodded.

Dor swiped a hand down her face. "Will it ever go away, what we did?"

"We need to hope so, because I can't keep living like this."

Dor hung her head. "Me neither."

PC Bob Holworth didn't know what to do next. Those two pains up his arse, Karen Scholes and Sharon Barnett, had offered to help him with that man going missing, but nothing had come of their good turn. He'd been surprised they'd mentioned doing a flyer, considering they didn't like 'pigs' as he'd heard them refer to the police one night in The Donny. Were they up to something? Did he need to be on his guard?

The thing was, Bob had been warned by The Pains to mind his own business when it came to scraps on the estate—or anything else for that matter. Then there was that bloke, an up-and-coming gangster type, Lenny Grafton, having a word in Bob's shell-like that things were going to change one day, and unless Bob toed the line, there'd be trouble.

What that change was and when it would happen hadn't been revealed, and Bob didn't really want to know. The problem was, the Barrington was his beat route, as well as the town centre, and he couldn't very well look the other way too often else his sergeant would wonder why the estate had suddenly calmed down.

But on saying that… Bob could make out he had it so under control that no one dared break the law anymore. Then, went this Lenny fella did whatever it was he had planned, the sergeant wouldn't have to know anything about it.

Nodding, Bob left Vera's B&B, content he'd looked down all avenues and couldn't proceed further. Steve Zander was just one of many missing people in the country, and his family would have to accept he'd taken himself off to start again elsewhere.

Chuffed he'd put that episode to bed—well, almost, he had paperwork to fill out yet—he checked his watch and, seeing as it was five minutes after his shift ended, he got in the patrol car and drove back to the station.

Case closed.

Chapter Twenty-Two

Cassie woke after sleeping for twelve hours straight. Groggy, she got out of bed and went into the bathroom to shower and whatnot. Once dressed, she met Mam in the kitchen and sat at the island. Mam took a plate of full English out of the microwave and placed it in front of Cassie.

"I heard you get up so warmed it for you." Mam smiled and picked up a cup of coffee, passing that along, too. "A late night for you then."

Cassie nodded and cut some bacon. "I killed Jason. Took him to Marlene. Ted and Felix dealt with him after that. Jimmy was with me."

"How did he cope?" Mam propped a hip against the island.

"Pretty well, considering. Until he puked when the mince came out of the machine." Cassie ate the bacon, unperturbed that she chewed cooked meat while discussing raw.

Mam chuckled. "Poor sod. He'll get used to it. I take it you *will* be using him in future."

Cassie nodded. "That reminds me, I have to nip twenty K round to him in a bit. I'll get it from of the safe on my way out."

"Ah, the sum for murder. I thought you said *you'd* killed Jason."

"I did, but I wanted Jimmy to see what he could earn just by being involved. Once he's done whatever he needs to with that money, plus the five hundred a week for being my ears, he'll want more, no matter what he has to do to get it. They all start off boffing then change their tune once they have cash to flash."

"Hmm."

Cassie ate her breakfast while Mam got up and loaded the dishwasher. Cassie should feel bad for enticing Jimmy, using him like this when he wasn't that way inclined, but she didn't trust many people and needed someone on hand to do whatever she asked. She thought of Shirl. Jimmy had asked whether he could talk to her about things, and Cassie had agreed, reinforcing the rule that if Shirl blabbed, she was dead meat.

Jimmy had more than got the point, seeing as he'd so recently puked about the mince.

She'd have to get to his flat soon as the February Fayre started today. Sharon had taken over the running of it with gusto, according to Brenda's latest WhatsApp report, which Cassie had read when she'd flopped into bed, exhausted.

Her mind strayed back to last night and Jimmy. He'd had several shocks but had coped well. He was definitely someone she wanted on her close team, especially with Jason no longer around to do the dirty work, although Jimmy wasn't quite ready to torture people in the squat for her. Maybe Glen Maddock fancied doing that for some extra cash. He didn't strike her as the sort who'd settle into retirement without getting bored.

Once Jason's mince filled one and a half tubs, she'd guided Jimmy out of the side room, leaving the cousins to clean Marlene and take the meat to Handel Farm. In the corridor, she'd told Jimmy to go home, get some rest, while she visited the squat to burn Jason's clothing, and her own.

Crew Two had been there when she'd arrived, the carpet already rolled up by the two fellas, a woman on the floor scrubbing the boards, another wiping a wall. Cassie had changed into clean leggings and a top from her boot, made them hot drinks once she'd fed the furnace, then got down on her knees to help wash the nasty wallpaper in the living room, still too wired up to go home and sleep. The crew had chatted as if they weren't ridding the place of blood, and Cassie found out a lot by listening to them.

It had felt good to be a part of the team instead of the leader of it.

Breakfast finished, she sipped some coffee. "Thanks for that, Mam."

"I thought you'd need it. You've hardly eaten the last couple of days."

"Been *slightly* busy." She resisted rolling her eyes. "How was Lou after I left?"

Mam squirted the worktops and hob with anti-bacterial spray. "She should crawl back into her hole now. I had a word, let her know any more shit for us to deal with, and we won't be happy."

"How did she take it?"

"Okay, actually." Mam wiped the sides with a sponge. "Said she'd better get cracking making the pies for the Fayre, so she'd be baking well into the early hours."

"She'll have been awake when Felix and Ted turned up then."

"Hmm. How did Jimmy handle knowing what Marlene is?"

Cassie smiled. "I think he was a bit shocked but relieved he didn't have to meet some nutter."

"I'll never forget when Doreen first twigged it was the mincer."

It seemed ages ago now that Doreen had killed Karen, yet it was so recent. The pigs' murders had wiped away the shit with Karen and Zhang Wei, then dealing with Jason had stolen more time, stretching it so it felt as if weeks had gone by. Hopefully, there'd be no hassle for a while now. Cassie and Mam could enjoy the two days of the Fayre and kick back for a bit, Cassie only doing the usual estate business, collecting rents, managing the drugs, and all the other little things that made up her daily routine.

"Right, I'd better get down to Jimmy's then the Fayre, show my face, wave the collection box for Gorley's funeral flowers under their noses to take suspicion off us." She stood. "Are you coming with me or going in your own car?"

"I'll be down in a bit."

Cassie went into the hallway then the office to take some cash out of the safe, ignoring the ledger that needed filling out. Work could do one for now. She put the money in her purse and, back in the hallway, stuck her boots on, slid her arms into her jacket sleeves, and zipped it up.

Excitement from childhood swirled inside her at the thought of the Fayre, although she doubted the candy floss and hot dogs would appeal to her now, but she could sniff them in the air and remember her times at Sculptor's Field with Dad, up on his shoulders, him letting her down when she wanted to go on the merry-go-round, and she always, always chose the unicorn to sit on, pretending she was a fairy.

She drove away feeling lighter now Lou had earnt the title of The Piggy Farmer and Jason was out of the picture. Amazing really, how much he'd annoyed her just by breathing. With him dead, a weight had sloughed off her shoulders, and life had gone back to normal. Well, it would once Branding closed the cases on Gorley, Knight, and Codderidge.

Cassie dropped Jimmy's cash off, not staying to chat, then drove to Sculptor's Field. She parked in the cordoned-off area reserved for cars, of which there were many. The weather hadn't prevented people from coming out—it never did for the Fayre—and most of the snow had gone, only the cold air remaining plus a weird white sky, no clouds. Dad would have predicted more snow was on the way, but the weatherman, chortling on the radio last night as she'd driven home, had said otherwise. Tomorrow, the sun was coming, along with milder days for a week or so, a fake spring making an appearance.

She approached the Fayre, as giddy as a young girl at the sight of the tents and stalls set out in a massive circle on the frozen ground, people milling around on the grass in the enclosed area, The Beast towering high above them right in the middle of it all.

It resembled a market in a horseshoe shape, but at the top was Clive the Clown's red-and-white-striped tent, the largest, with its white ball on top, same as a newel post. To either side, just behind, were purple-and-white ones, flags flapping in the breeze. The medium one on the right belonged to Betty's daughter, Liz, who'd taken over Bloom's once her mother had died, and the smallest, to the left, was the somewhat eerie weekend home to The Old Mystic.

Times past, Cassie had wanted to go in, but of course, Dad had said no, she was too small for the likes of fortunes being told and, "You don't want to be believing anything that comes out of that baggage's mouth. She speaks a right load of horseshit—and don't tell Mam I swore."

Now, though, she could make her own decisions and, as she walked through the crowd, nodding at anyone who dared to make eye contact, she headed straight for the little tent.

Sod's law, Doreen stopped her.

"All right, duck?"

"Fine, ta. Finally got some breathing space." Cassie smiled. "Everything's been put to bed. Well, everything I can manage anyroad."

"Good. I've just been having a natter with Lou. She said she's been busy lately, made a point of saying it, too, but that she'd come and find me in a bit to talk about some things she has on her mind."

"Well, she won't be busy anymore." *What's on her mind? The murders? Is she planning to tell Doreen?*

"Oh." Doreen folded her hands over her belly, her coat open, showing a white blouse beneath. "I won't pry." She pointed to the knitted willy warmer stall. "Brenda's over there. Said she'd be talking to you about her client on Monday."

"Right." Cassie's shoulders slumped. There couldn't be a problem else Brenda would have WhatsApped, but the mention of work had erased some of her good mood. Couldn't she have just *one* day where it wasn't mentioned? "Well, I'm off to see The Old Mystic for a laugh."

"I wouldn't joke about her." Doreen sucked her lower lip. "She's a right creepy one, she is. I went to see her, God, must be a decade ago now, at her house, you know, so no one knew I'd gone. She told me a few things I'd kept a secret, and I fair shit myself, I did."

"So you think she actually knows things?"

"She does, although she couldn't tell my future for some reason, only my past. If you're still of a mind to chat to her, be warned, you might come out a different person." Doreen patted Cassie's arm. "Speak to you soon." She walked away, vanishing into a huddle of people close to The Beast.

Cassie shivered, remaining in place. Should she go and see Mystic? There were so many things she wanted to ask about Dad, but then again, she couldn't if she wanted his mistakes to remain hidden.

Maybe she knows about them already.

Cassie pulled herself upright and walked on with a 'no one tells me what to do' attitude, skirting around the pegs in the ground from the ropes on Clive the Clown's tent, then pausing in front of Mystic's. The flap was closed, so someone must be inside. Cassie read the whiteboard easel with a poster stuck to it stating the prices.

CRYSTAL BALL: £10

PALM READING: £20

TAROT CARDS: £25

SOUL SEARCHING: £50

Soul Searching? What the hell was that?

"I know you're out there, Cassie Grafton."

Cassie jumped, looking around, then eyed the flap. It didn't have any gaps in it, so how the hell had Mystic seen her?

"Come in. Soul Searching is what you need. A nudge to let you know your thoughts and emotions are telling you something."

Dread swirled in the pit of Cassie's stomach, and she turned to walk away, needing to surround herself with people instead of feeling vulnerable and alone while a disembodied voice spoke to her.

"If you walk away, you'll make the biggest mistake of your life."

She paused, her breath catching. The voice was wizened, strong yet calm, coming from a woman who commanded respect and inspired fear. Cassie hadn't bothered visiting her when she'd taken over from Dad, the only resident she'd steered clear of to let them know she was in charge—Mam had advised her to leave the old woman be. Now, Cassie wished she'd ignored the advice and introduced herself so at least she wouldn't be afraid. And she *was* afraid. Despite her bravado, the fear *she* inspired in people, she was uneasy.

She glanced around. Typical. No one stood nearby, not even any kiddies wanting to see Clive, although laughter and clapping abruptly rang out inside his big top; the clown must be doing a show. Liz sat behind one of the tables in her tent, head bowed as she created a bouquet, and while Cassie could walk over there and ignore Mystic's command, she didn't.

She reached out and drew the flap across, expecting a pentagram sprayed on the grass inside, candles lighting the place, a creepy vibe going on, but it was nothing like that. Two purple wingback armchairs sat adjacent to one another, a table in front of one, the top pulled over Mystic's blanket-covered legs. A tall standard lamp with a purple velvet shade, tassels dangling, stood behind her, lighting the woman in a scarlet glow from what must be a red bulb. To the rear of the other chair, another lamp with a normal light, although it was low and only illuminated the seat. Cassie stepped inside and let the flap go, and the immense feeling of being trapped came over her.

She wanted to run.

"If you do, the past will only chase you," Mystic whispered. "Better to be forewarned than go forth unaware."

Cassie cocked a hip, allowing her monster to stretch its legs, preparing herself to give the woman a piece of her mind for intimidating her like this. She opened her mouth to speak.

"You, *or* Lenny's creature inside you, don't bother me, Grafton." Mystic, her white wiry hair, long and spread out on her shoulders, beckoned her forward with a knobbly-knuckled hand, the fingers resembling claws, the nails silver talons. "Sit. Listen." She paused. "And learn."

Drawn to the other chair, Cassie obeyed.

"Money must cross my palm before we enter into the realm of the Unknown, its full title The Unknown to You, because you don't have the gift. It's known to me. I'm told things, sometimes after the fact, sometimes before."

Cassie took her purse from her jacket pocket, pissed off that she trembled. She snatched out fifty quid and placed it in Mystic's outstretched hand.

Mystic curled the notes into her fist—they crackled—then stuffed the money down the side of the seat cushion. "Knowing everything beforehand means I see outcomes, and if it turns out for the good, I remain silent. With Jess... She was supposed to be returned, but outside influences got in the way, as is sometimes the will of destiny and fate. I didn't know who'd murdered her until after Brenda discovered it was Vance—The Unknown to You didn't show me. It's a veiled place, where people's secrets are waiting to be discovered, and spirits remain close-lipped until they have a mind to pass them on."

"What did you mean when you said if I walk away it'll be my biggest mistake?"

Mystic smiled, her dark irises even darker from the red bulb. "What did you think I meant?"

Frustrated, Cassie barked, "Walking away from this fucking tent, what else?"

"It's foolhardy to assume."

Cassie sighed.

Mystic's smile vanished. "What I *meant* was, if you walk away from the Barrington."

"Why would I do *that*?"

Laughter rasped out of the old woman. "Don't pretend you've never thought about it. The business, it's harder than you thought. Your feelings on being who you've become are harder to understand than you thought. There's more *murder* than you thought."

That was true, but how did Mystic know? Did the ghosts from that shitty Unknown place tell her this? For God's sake, ghosts didn't even exist, so this silly cow must be guessing.

"I never guess." Mystic reached down the side of the chair and brought out a purple cloth. She flapped it so it billowed up then landed on the table. Next, she fished for a crystal ball.

"I'm not bloody paying you another tenner," Cassie said, aggrieved the old bat wanted to scam her.

"It's in the Soul Searching price. *Tsk*. So quick to judge; a downfall, perhaps."

Cassie ignored her and waited while the creepy tart stared into the ball of glass held aloft, the only thing inside it Mystic's skewed face from the other side. No revelations playing out, no swirling mist or floating clouds. Like Dad had said, Cassie certainly *didn't* want to believe anything that came out of this baggage's mouth.

"Yet Lenny Grafton believed it all, because I proved I spoke the truth." Mystic lowered the ball.

What? Dad had gone to see her? And how is she reading my mind?

"He visited me. I see he didn't tell you, nor did he write it in his coded books." Mystic put the ball away. "I've confirmed with the Unknown that something will happen today, a murder, but I don't know who the killer is."

For God's sake, another murder? "Convenient."

"So you might think. If I knew, I'd tell you…I think." Mystic paused. "And those pigs…"

Cassie's stomach rolled over; she was super uncomfortable now. "What pigs?"

"You can pretend with others but not with me. The four police officers. It'll go away, courtesy of the paid pig. What you must concern yourself with now is this. Someone's getting too big for their boots—not like Jason or Karen, and not like Zhang Wei."

"How did you find out about that?"

Mystic continued. "This person will cause problems, and it's all to do with the well."

"The well?"

Mystic mumbled some garbled words, eyes closed. Her lashes fluttered, then she stared straight at Cassie. "Never give the Barrington up. If you do, everyone will suffer. No matter how much it tests you, keep the crown. And it *will* test you. Many times over."

Cassie's pulse throbbed in her neck.

"What you thought about nature versus nurture." Mystic sucked in a long breath. "It's nurture. Lenny made you who you are."

Cassie couldn't handle that truth so changed the subject. "What about the murder? Who is it? Can I stop it from happening? Or is it me who's going to kill someone?"

Mystic gasped and clutched her stomach.

Cassie's heart skipped a beat. "What's the matter?"

"I am afraid the knife has already entered. Once, twice, three times. And again. Again."

Cassie shot up and yanked the flap across. It was so bright outside compared to the murk of the tent, and she blinked to see properly. Liz was serving a customer, and kids with their parents streamed out of Clive's tent, yapping excitedly. Cassie ran forward, heading for the crowd, everyone still mooching about, chatting or standing at stalls. Someone cheered on the Hook the Duck, a yellow duck dangling on the end of a wooden rod, water dripping.

She ran to the right, planning to make a circuit of the inner horseshoe, seeking out anyone who'd been stabbed. On she went, searching the six people at the tombola, then glanced at Sharon doing the face-painting. A little girl smiled, her skin lilac, Sharon putting a black butterfly on her cheek, the mother hovering nearby.

Cassie rushed on, reaching the bottom then going up the other side. Lou bustled in through the back of her pie and jam stall, handing over a jar of blackberry to a customer, the lid red-and-white checks. A weird, cracked icing figure with blonde hair was propped against one of the pies, in pink wellies and a tutu, Lou saying, "What a good little girl you are."

How *insane* it was to notice that when panic ruled. Cassie moved along, darting around people waiting for the merry-go-round, the piped music she'd loved as a child grating on her nerves. The other stalls had nothing much going on, so she spun to survey the throng in the middle.

Nothing was happening.

Mystic's full of bollocks.

A scream pierced the air above the conversations, then another, longer and shriller, and the Fayre-goers hushed, turning a one-eighty to see who'd cried out. Cassie did the same, and it didn't take long to find where the commotion was. At the top of the horseshoe, in front of the hot dog van, people parted, stepping away from something or someone, a girl screaming again, holding her temples, a man wrapping an arm around her and leading her away. Cassie forged ahead, her heart beating so loud, adrenaline bringing on speed, and she stopped dead when she reached the space.

Blood coated a woman's midriff, her hand clutched to it, red, so red, scarlet pouring so fast she must have been stabbed several times. *'Once, twice, three times. And again. Again.'* Where had she been between Mystic saying the knife had already entered and now? Behind the hot dog van? In Clive's tent? No, she wouldn't have been in there, she had no little kids.

"Help me, Cass. Oh God, help me..." The woman stretched her other hand out, blood dripping from her mouth, her eyes rolling.

This couldn't be happening. It couldn't.

The crowd seemed to disappear, and all that was left was Cassie and the stabbed lady, all sounds fading apart from the victim's stuttered breathing and Cassie's shallow gasps, then:

"What the fuck?" A man.

"Oh shit, she's been stabbed!" A teenager.

"Someone call an ambulance!"

"Already did."

Then they faded, and the woman reached Cassie, grabbing at her coat collar, dropping to her knees. She stared up, straight into Cassie's eyes, hers filling.

"Tell me who did this to you," Cassie said.

"It's too late," the lady whispered, blood bubbling. "Too late."

Cassie went down with her, pushing her onto her back then taking her jacket off, pressing it to the injury. "It'll be okay, I promise it'll be okay."

"You can't…fix…everything."

"I've got to try." Cassie let out a sob, not caring who saw her as weak. "I can't let you die."

"You're going to…have to…let me…go." She closed her eyes.

"No! Don't you *dare* go to sleep." Cassie pressed harder, helpless, unable to mend this terrible thing.

"Thanks...for the...perfume, duck. Best...present of...my life."

Tears blinded Cassie, and she let them fall, knowing, in her heart of hearts, that no ambulance would save her new friend.

Doreen Prince was gone.

To be continued in The Barrington Patch 4

The Old Mystic

Printed in Great Britain
by Amazon